ANITBEET PRODUCTIONS PRESENTS:

A Thug's Redemption 2:

Jamal's Return

Yani

After being away from his neighborhood for more than nine years and finding a career as a Wilmington Delaware Police Detective, Jamal is lured back to North Philly when a shoot-out erupts, killing one of his best friends. A Detective, who becomes familiar with Jamal's past, unravels shocking truths about drugs, dirty cops, and their role in a drug war that is claiming lives in a North Philly neighborhood, daily. Jamal is blackmailed and forced into a position to possibly take down his cousin Samir. Now faced with a matter of kill or be killed, Jamal must decide whether he will return to his life from the past, or honor his badge. In this urban fiction sequel, all bets are off and everyone, including Jamal, is expendable!

Dedication

In my last book, I dedicated it to the many lives lost. So many more have been lost between the first release of *A Thug's Redemption*, and this one. This book will be dedicated to the survivors, to the people who continue to push forward day in and day out despite the disruption, the violence, the drama and the endless battle for peace in inner cities across the country. We must show the world that we are more than what the media portrays us to be. We must show that we can persevere no matter how many obstacles are placed before us. This battle for peace and to cease the violence that we commit against our own kind will not be won by political figures stepping in to save us. It can only be won when WE have the courage to fight our way out and save ourselves. Blessings and peace to all of my readers and supporters!

I also want to dedicate this book to Tierra Brown for being one of my biggest supporters and my most eager reader, encouraging me to write more. Your enthusiasm moved me, motivated me and inspired me more than you know. Thank you so much, my Gemini Twin. And to Bryheem (Turtle) Bryant, how could I not shout out my "partner in crime"? From a distance, you helped me more than you can imagine. To my sister, Sharmon Mitchell; thank you for coming to my book signings, sitting through them to keep me company and helping me haul those heavy boxes of my books. You are truly the bomb dot com! To my other Gemini Twin, Celia Green, who sat up many nights listening to me obsess over the plot of this story, who dreamed with me, dreamed for me and believed in me more than I believed in myself sometimes. Thanks so much for all of the endless conversations and being my back up brain when my own would burn out from exhaustion. I always have to thank the best bombdiggity mom in the entire world, Betty Bunn. I hope I continue to make you proud. To my cover designer, Rashad Campbell: thanks for turning out the bomb cover design! And lastly my little mini mes; Destiny and Demetrius: Let my work ethic inspire you to be greater than what I aspire to be. I do this for the both of you. There would be no me without the two of you. "*…we're tired of turning the other cheek while they (thugs) destroy our neighborhoods, kill our men, rape our women and leave our children fatherless and unprotected. It's a vicious cycle that needs to stop! We can't expect political figures to come in and correct our shit if we're not willing to correct it ourselves. It starts with us first!*" – Keisha Brown. A Thug's Redemption 2: Jamal's Return

1

On an unusually warm day in early November of 2011, Manny was hanging on the corner of 24th and Oxford Street with his older brother Kiree and their best friend D-Ball. Manny had just turned 26 and was making plans to have a big birthday party at Luxe Lounge in the Old City section of Philadelphia. Times had been good for Manny and business had been booming for both he and his brother. They had become large over the years in the hustling game and were making more money than they could have ever imagined. Manny had promised his girlfriend Keisha of ten years that he would stop hustling for the sake of their son Kamir, but jobs were scarce and there was no way he was going to see his family go without.

The sun was shining and a warm breeze blew litter and leaves around that had fallen from the trees. Manny unzipped his hooded sweat-shirt to invite the breeze in to cool off a bit, not anticipating it to be such a warm day. He looked at his watch to see what time it was as he had promised Keisha earlier that he would pick her up from work and they would all go out to dinner. "It's nice as shit out here today," he said to his older brother as he leaned into the wall of the corner Papi store.

"Yeah, I don't trust weather like this. Whenever the sun comes out, niggas get stupid. I hope I don't have to fuck anybody up today." D-Ball said as he peered up the street.

"Nah, everything has been calm since we made that truce with Samir. These Young Heads don't wanna go to war with us let alone Sa." Kiree said in response.

"I guess," Manny replied. "But you know some Young Head that just scored his first big pay and seen one too many *Paid in Full* type movies is going to start feeling himself."

Kiree chuckled. "*Paid in Full*," he mocked. "You're funny as shit for that one. How's my Lil' Man doing? I ain't seen my nephew in over a month. Tell Keisha to make time to stop by."

"I will. She's just been so busy with the gig at Prudential and with my son. But we'll come through this weekend." Manny replied.

"One thing I can say about Keisha; that girl is a straight rider. She's been down with you since she was a young buck in the 9th grade. I never thought y'all would've lasted this long. You need to stop bull shitting and marry that girl. You know that's what mommy wants," Kiree said to his younger brother.

"Oh trust me, I plan on it. I'm just waiting for the right moment. Trying to put some plans into motion first, but I'ma put a ring on her finger real soon," Manny replied. He looked at a car that passed by and began to feel uneasy. He could have sworn that he had just seen the same car ride pass them two other times.

"Yeah, ya'll better. I got some toys for Lil' Man, too." Kiree replied.

"Oh that's what's up. Aye yo, bro; that dark green Bonneville that just passed by, I could've sworn that it rode through here a couple of times before already," Manny said as he looked down the street.

Kiree thought for a moment. "Nah, it's so many niggas around here riding in Bonnies. That's like the North Philly car; that and Crown Vics and Lesabres. Sometimes you're too paranoid."

D-Ball shook his head. "Nah, I peeped that shit, too. They came through three times."

"Yeah, paranoid my ass," Manny replied. "Fuck that, I'd rather be a moving target than a sitting duck, you feel me? I told Keisha I'd bring her some snacks. Let me grab them real quick and then we're out."

"I know that's the fuck right," D-Ball replied.

Manny went into the Papi store and grabbed the snacks that his girlfriend asked for. He stopped at the doorway to look at the cover of the Daily News and then walked out of the store when it happened. The same Bonneville sped around the corner and two guys jumped out opening fire without hesitation. D-Ball dove behind a car while Kiree took two to the chest and one to the stomach. Manny reached for his gun but was too slow. He took a shot in his shoulder and scrambled back inside of the store.

"MANNY!!" Kiree screamed out as blood poured from his mouth.

D-Ball peeked from behind the car that was shielding him and fired three shots at the gunmen. He missed and cursed himself. He could see Kiree crumpled on the ground in a fetal position.

Manny pulled his gun and fired shots out of the store. D-Ball wasn't the target; the hit was for Manny and Kiree. Samir wanted them taken out as soon as possible, so the gunmen moved towards the store not wanting to be distracted.

"MANNY!" Kiree managed to squeal again.

"KIREE!! KIREE! Hold on baby!" Manny called back to his brother. He scooted back so he could see who came into the store before they saw him.

D-Ball was almost in a panic. He knew if he didn't move fast, both of his friends would be killed. He pulled his back up pistol from his pants and tapped them together.

"Fuck this," he growled. He wasn't going out like a nut and swore he wasn't going alone either. He jumped up and fired both guns at the gunmen. One turned to fire back and took a shot to the head. The other gunman ran into the store in part to hide and in part to finish off Manny. They saw each other at the same time. Manny fired his gun just as the gunman fired his. He caught two shots to his chest but got a lucky shot off that hit his target in the neck. D-Ball ran into the store and shot the gunman in the head, finishing him off. He then ran over to Manny.

"Manny, are you good?" D-Ball asked as he knelt beside him trembling. He could hear him taking shallow breaths. He cursed and looked around. He figured the owners were hiding in the back and had already called 9-1-1. The police could be there any minute and he didn't want to get caught. "I'm sorry; Manny…I'm so sorry. I gotta go. Just hold on, homie. I swear I'ma find out who's responsible for this shit." D-Ball ran from the store, jumped into his car and sped off just as the sounds of sirens were drawing near.

2

Detective Davidson stopped his car away from the scene. He was used to the scenery. Almost every other day, some poor, young, black male was being gunned down on the streets of North Philly. It was becoming a pattern and he had suspected a turf war was erupting. He lifted the caution tape and ducked underneath so he could begin his investigation. Two bodies lay outside covered with a white sheet. Davidson walked over to the one closest to the Bonneville.

"Who's the victim?" he asked a uniformed cop that was standing nearby.

"I dunno. He didn't have any ID on him. But judging by the ski-mask that's on his face, I'm assuming he was the aggressor."

"Or an extra for a Batman movie," Davidson joked to lighten the mood. He stepped over the body and made his way to the second body by the side wall of the corner store. He pulled the sheet back and his heart sank into his stomach.

"This guy had ID on him, uhh Kiree…" the officer started to say.

"…Stephens. Yeah… I know him. I grew up with him and his younger brother…"

The uniformed officer interrupted him. "Emmanuel Stephens?"

Davidson looked up at him. "Yeah, why?"

"Well we found him in the store. It looks like he took two GSW's to the chest and one to the shoulder. We found a gun next to him and a fourth body not too far from him also wearing a ski mask. He appears to have a fatal GSW to the head and one to the neck. We're waiting for ballistics to run some information to us. Judging by the angle of the head shot, I'm betting there's another shooter missing from the action," the uniformed officer concluded.

Davidson stood straight up. "You tell ballistics to put a rush on those results. I want them in my hands now. No, not now, but right damn it now. We have four dead victims and a missing gunman."

"No sir, three dead victims, one in critical; Emmanuel was rushed to Temple University Hospital listed in critical condition. There's no other info on him, yet," the officer corrected.

Davidson shook his head. "Un-fucking-believable. Manny, you better damn it make it. You have a son, a girlfriend. I can't even imagine how to break this news to their mother. Has the mother been notified?"

"Not that I am aware of, sir. Would you like for me to send a couple of guys over to reach out to her?"

"No… I'll handle it." Davidson looked around. He had been keeping record of the recent shootings in the area and noticed a pattern with the way the shootings occurred, the times, and the way all of the victims were tied to each other. This was definitely more than random gun violence in North Philly. This was a drug war. One thing he concluded after going over ballistic reports to recent shootings is they all had one thing in common; the soldiers fighting this drug war were armed with weapons only cops were supposed to have. He had suspected for a while that there were dirty cops on the force. He had seen something similar years ago when he was a rookie.

"I'm taking it that none of these beautiful people out here saw what happened?" Davidson asked sarcastically.

"You got it. Didn't see shit, don't know shit. And what's worse is the damn store didn't have tapes in the damn surveillance cameras."

Davidson closed his eyes and chuckled angrily. "Who the fuck has a corner store across the street from the got damn projects in the heart of the hood and don't put tapes in the got damn surveillance cameras? Only at the Papi store. Jesus H. Christ!" He kicked a trashcan over in anger drawing attention from other cops. "You call the lab and tell them I want those results now!" he growled.

"Yes sir," the uniformed cop stuttered as he moved away to do as he was told.

Davidson stood for a moment looking around. Kiree had been a good friend of his. He had warned him over the years that the street life only had a back door and a front door: one leading to the grave or the other leading to a jail cell. He would've rather seen him judged by twelve and not carried by six. He prayed that his younger brother wouldn't be joining him. Something had to give and soon.

Davidson suddenly had a thought. He walked back to his car and grabbed his phone. "Yeah, Wilmington Police Department, this is Detective Keith Davidson from the 22nd District here in Philadelphia. I need to get in touch with one of your detectives by the name of Jamal Williams…"

3

Keisha stood in the lobby of Prudential Bank in the Center City section of Philadelphia with one of her co-workers. She was new at the job, only working there for five months after graduating from West Chester University and felt on top of the world. She was still with the love of her life, Manny. They had a four year old son together and an awesome apartment in the Jenkintown section of Philadelphia. Everything was going smoothly and she couldn't be happier. She was showing pictures of her son to her co-worker, laughing and joking when she happened to look at the clock and saw that it was almost 5:30PM. "Are you sure your boyfriend isn't going to mind giving me a ride? I don't want to put y'all out the way," her co-worker asked her.

"Oh no, it's cool. Manny isn't like that. He would rather give you a ride home and make sure that you got there safely than have you get on a bus or train and something happens to you," Keisha replied as she tucked the photos inside of her black leather Tory Burch clutch handbag that Manny recently purchased for her. She grabbed her phone to call Manny. "He's a little late. Normally he's on time or would call me if he's going to be late." She noticed that her phone was off and chuckled. "I was about to have a whole attitude that he didn't call me and my silly ass forgot to turn my phone on when I left my desk." The two girls laughed together.

"So, how long have you two been together?" her co-worker asked her.

"We've been together since September 2001," Keisha replied as she waited for her new iPhone to load.

"Wow girl!! That's a long time. What's your secret because I'm lucky if I can keep a man for six months?" They laughed together.

"Love and trust; that's really all I can tell you. I love that man with all of my heart. He's done some things that I don't really agree with, but I understand the method to his madness. And he's always been good to me. When I got pregnant with our son, he made sure I still finished school and got my degree. I don't know what I would do without him," Keisha said quietly. After her phone loaded up, she saw she had multiple text messages and voicemails. Instead of reading them, she called Manny's phone. It rang until it went to voicemail.

"Hey babe, where are you? I'm in the lobby of my job waiting for you. Did we make other plans and I forgot? Call me when you get this. I'm going to walk over to the Juicy Couture shop and look around. I love you…" Keisha disconnected the call and looked at her phone.

"Is everything okay?" Keisha's co-worker asked.

"Yeah…" Keisha replied quietly. "This isn't like him at all." She began scanning her text messages to see who they were from. She saw that she had five from her best friend Angela saying in all caps to call her ASAP. Just as she was about to call her to see what the problem was, Angela was calling her.

"Hey girl, what's up?" Keisha answered.

"Why the fuck weren't you answering your phone? Didn't you hear my voicemails???" Angela shrieked into the phone.

"Why are you yelling and cursing? My phone was off at my desk. I forgot to turn it back on. What the hell are you so hype for?"

"THEY KILLED KIREE!!!" Angela yelled in tears.

"What?!" Keisha replied feeling weak. Her heart was pounding in her chest. "What? What do you mean? When?!"

"Not even an hour ago! Manny's in the hospital, too! They don't know if he's going to make it. They said he got hit like four times!" Angela said, hysterically.

"Oh my God!" Keisha said instantly in tears. She fell to the floor crying. Her co-worker crouched next to her to console her.

"What's wrong? What happened?" she asked Keisha.

"They shot my boyfriend and killed his brother!" Keisha screamed.

"Oh my God!" she snatched the phone from Keisha. "Hi, this is Liz, Keisha's co-worker. What hospital is he in? I'll get her there as soon as I can... Temple University Hospital? Okay, we're on our way." She disconnected the call and flagged down the security guard who was already making his way to them, noticing that something was wrong.

"It's going to be okay, Keisha. Just hang in there," Liz said trying to help Keisha get a hold of herself. Keisha wasn't hearing her. She wasn't hearing anything. How could her world be so perfect and then shatter in a matter of seconds?

"Is everything alright?" the security guard asked.

Yani

"I need a cab, now! She just found out her son's father was shot and his brother was killed." Liz explained as she helped Keisha stand up.

The security guard ran to the door and flagged down a cab that was coming around the corner. He helped Liz get Keisha into the car and instructed the driver where to go.

On the way there, Keisha's phone was going off back to back with phone calls and text messages from everyone. She was losing her mind as she thought her worst nightmare was becoming a harsh reality. It didn't seem like the cab was moving fast enough.

"Can't you drive any faster man, come on!!" Keisha pleaded in tears.

"I'm driving as fast as I can, considering this is rush hour," the cab driver responded nervously.

"Drive faster, jump lights, just get me to Temple Hospital, now!"

Liz threw her arm around Keisha and pulled her close. "I'm sorry sir, can you just please step on it?"

When they arrived, Liz paid the driver as Keisha bolted through the hospital doors. A security guard grabbed her.

"M'am, m'am, slow down. What can I do for you?" he asked her.

"My boyfriend uh, Emmanuel Stephens; he was brought here an hour ago. He was shot. I need to see him," Keisha said as she trembled. Angela ran over to Keisha and threw her arms around her. They cried together.

The security guard ushered them over to a nurse's station. "Do we have an Emmanuel Stephens here?"

The nurse began typing and looked on her computer screen. "Yes, he's in surgery."

"Is he okay?" Keisha asked through tear drenched eyes.

"I can't say m'am. You'll have to talk with the doctors. One of his friends and a little boy just went up. They are on the 12th floor in the waiting room," the nurse told her.

"Your brother is here. I called him when I finally got a hold of you," Angela said as she wiped Keisha's face.

"Maurice is here?" Keisha asked confused. She hadn't seen Maurice in over a year. They had a nasty falling out over his and Deisha's break up.

"Yeah, hurry up," Angela told her. She grabbed Keisha's arm and they ran over to the elevator with Liz in tow.

Yani

"What the hell happened? Who did this, Angie?" Keisha asked as she wiped her eyes.

Angela looked at Liz and then looked at Keisha to get the okay to speak. Keisha nodded her head. "I don't know. Moe told me it sounded like fucking Afghanistan out there. The two dudes that did it are dead though. Somebody else was with Manny and Kiree but he didn't say who."

"D-Ball…" Keisha mumbled.

"Yup, I was thinking the same thing. You know those three been thick as thieves since way back when and D-Ball always had their back," Angela agreed.

"Then why the fuck did he leave them there, huh? If he's supposed to be their best fucking friend how could he just let them get hit liked that?!" Keisha replied furiously.

"That's not what happened. From what Moe told me, Manny would be dead if it wasn't for D-Ball. Well… he didn't say D-Ball was there but we all know he was."

They arrived to their floor and Keisha hurried down the hallway.

"Mommy!" she heard her son exclaim. He was sitting on Maurice's lap. He squirmed off and ran over to her cheerfully, oblivious to what was going on. Keisha scooped him up in her arms and held him tightly. She covered him with kisses and then put him down.

"Maurice…" Keisha said in tears as her brother wrapped his arms around her. They didn't need to say anything. They had been through this before when Dominique was killed. This time was much more tragic.

"I'm so sorry, Keesh. I came here as soon as I got the call," Maurice told her.

"Thank you," Keisha replied as she let him go. She looked around. "Where's Ms. Becky?"

Maurice hesitated. "Kiree was killed. She didn't take the news too well and had a heart attack."

Keisha covered her mouth. "Oh my God!" she squealed and burst into tears. "This shit is fucking wrong on too many levels. Where is Manny, now?"

"He's still in surgery. From what I was told he got hit twice in the chest, but I don't know what's good with him."

"I need you to do me a favor… two actually. Take my son out of here. If something happens to his father, I don't want him to see me crying," Keisha requested.

"You're sure? I understand why you're asking but you shouldn't be here by yourself," Maurice replied.

"I'll be okay. I have Liz and Angie with me and I'm sure more of Kiree and Manny's family will be here, soon. But I don't want him to know what's going on."

"Okay. I got you. What's the other favor?"

Keisha leaned over and whispered in Maurice's ear. "Call Jamal and tell him to find D-Ball and find his ass now."

"Why?" Maurice asked in a low tone. Keisha knelt in front of her son, Kamir. "Kay-baby, I want you to sit with Auntie Angie while I talk to your Uncle Mar, okay?"

"Okay mommy," Kamir replied. Angela took his hand and led him over to the vending machine to buy him a bag of chips and a juice.

Keisha grabbed Maurice by the hand and pulled him over to a corner where they could talk in private.

"What does Jamal have to do with anything and why do you need him to find D-Ball?" Maurice asked.

"Isn't Jamal a cop now?" Keisha asked.

"Yeah but he would be way out of jurisdiction. He's not with the Philadelphia Police Department. He's out Delaware."

"I don't care. Kiree was one of his best friends. I'm sure there's something he can do. I know it is." The anger was present in Keisha's face.

"Keesh, is there something you're not telling me?"

"Manny and Kiree just made a truce with Samir supposedly. I heard Manny tell Kiree that he didn't trust it but I didn't hear him say why. But he kept stressing that he had a feeling Samir was trying to get them to let their guard down. Now Kiree is dead and Manny is fighting for his life. It doesn't take a fucking genius to see who's behind this," Keisha seethed through clenched teeth.

"Wait a minute hold up, Manny was still hustling even after y'all had Kamir? What the fuck was he thinking knowing how fucked up Samir is? You and Kamir could've been in danger!" Maurice replied angrily.

"Maurice, please don't start. We can argue that shit later," Keisha said as she shook her head.

"Fine, whatever. I still don't get what D-Ball has to do with this?"

"Both of the guys that shot Kiree and Manny were killed too," Keisha told her brother.

"You think D-Ball was there?" Maurice asked.
"You tell me when's the last time you saw Kiree and Manny and D-Ball wasn't around. I'm positive he was with them and was the one who killed the bastards that killed Kiree and shot Manny."

Maurice rubbed his hands across his face not liking the way this was sounding. "Okay, let's say that your theory is right, what does Jamal have to do with anything?"

"If the PPD finds out D-Ball was the one who killed those two guys, they are going to lock him up regardless if it was self-defense. Maybe Jamal can help him."

"Nah, D-Ball won't take help from Jamal let alone talk to him. Regardless of the fact that they were close friends, Jamal is a cop now. D-Ball ain't talking to him. But there's another problem. If you figured out D-Ball is always with Kiree and Manny and more than likely killed the guys that killed Kiree, Samir more than likely figured it out, too. They're going to be coming after D-Ball."

Keisha looked up at Maurice. "Shit…"

4

He could see her face as clear as day; her pretty light brown skin, her long dark hair and beautiful smile. She was radiant and as real as ever. She was standing in front of a mirror combing her hair and smiled at him. She then came over to the bed and playfully jumped in next to him. He could smell the vanilla and honey suckle scented body wash on her skin and feel her hand as she brushed it against his cheek. He could feel her cool breath as she leaned close to him to kiss him before saying, "I love you, Jamal."

"I love you too, Tammy…" He opened his eyes and like all of the dreams before, she was gone.

Jamal jumped up from his afternoon nap. "Tammy…?" he mumbled. He hadn't had a dream like that in over eight years. Why now? He closed his eyes as his heart began to ache. Though it had been more than nine years since the murder of Tamera and their daughter, he still missed her. He missed the life they were supposed to have but was robbed of. He missed what should've been but never was. He took a deep breath and swung his legs over the edge of the bed and touched the ring he still had of Tamera's. Out of habit, he played with it between his fingers before kissing it and then let it fall back against his chest.

Life was different for Jamal now. He made a career for himself on the right side of the law as a detective for the Wilmington Delaware Police. Outside of his brother, mother and best friend Maurice, he had pretty much severed ties with his past. He even managed to start a new relationship with a teacher from Thomas Edison Charter School, which was going pretty well for him. But Jamal knew from past experiences that when everything was going good, something was going to go wrong.

He noticed that the light on his cell phone was flashing. He checked it to see who it could be. He saw that he had a few missed calls from Maurice along with multiple missed calls from his Lieutenant at the station. He put his phone on speaker and let the messages play:

"Yo Jamal, this is Maurice. Call me when you get this. It's important. Peace."

"That was kinda vague homie," Jamal mumbled as he brushed his teeth.

"Hey Jamal, this is Sheila. I received an urgent request from a Detective Keith Davidson from the Philadelphia Police Department wanting to speak with you. He didn't say what it was about, but he claims it was important. Stop by my office when you come in."

"Who the hell is Keith Davidson?" Jamal mused. The name sounded sort of familiar but he wasn't sure. He definitely didn't like the idea of a Philly Detective seeking him out.

"Yo Jamal, I really need you to hit me up. You know I don't like putting things on voicemail. It's important homie. Hit me up."

Jamal looked at the phone. He didn't like the tone in Maurice's voice. He was starting to get the feeling that all was not kosher in his old neighborhood.

"Look Jamal I was hoping to get you on the phone but I know sometimes you turn anti-social and don't answer. Kiree was killed and Manny got hit, too. Get at me when you get this message."

Jamal's heart sank into his stomach. Not his homie Kiree Stephens! They had been best friends since they were two nappy-head nuccas running through the neighborhood, flipping on old mattresses and playing basketball with an old crate nailed to a pole posing as a basketball hoop. They went back more than 20 years. Not only was Kiree dead but Manny was caught, too? Something wasn't right.

"Yo Jamal, call me man. Keisha needs a favor. It would be even better if you could make it to Philly, ASAP. This ain't a conversation for the phone if you know what I mean…"

Jamal showered and got dressed. He was grabbing his phone and car keys when a call came through.

"Yes Lieutenant?" Jamal answered as he headed out of the door.

"Jamal, I've been getting calls from a Keith Davidson requesting to speak with you. He's not saying what it's about and I'm not too particular about Philly Cops seeking out my detectives. Do you know what this is about?"

Jamal hesitated. "I haven't the slightest clue," he said in a low tone.

"Yeah well call this guy back at your earliest convenience and nip whatever this is in the bud, okay?" she gave Jamal the phone number and Jamal stored it in his phone.

"Alright Lou, I'm on my way in." Jamal disconnected the call and put his blue tooth in his ear. He still couldn't get over the fact that Kiree was dead and his brother was fighting for his life. Who the hell was the detective that wanted to speak to him so badly? And why was Keisha asking for a favor? Something definitely was not right.

He called Maurice. "It's about time nigga, I thought maybe you cut me off too," Maurice answered without saying hello.

"What the hell is going on down there?" Jamal asked.

"Man, this shit is crazy. Kiree got murked, Manny is fighting for his life, Keisha is going out of her mind," Maurice replied.

"Yeah man, I got your messages. So what's up?"

"How soon can you get to Philly?"

Jamal took a deep breath. "Man… you know I don't come through there no more."

"Yeah I know and I wouldn't ask you if it wasn't important."

"Does this have to do with the favor Keisha is asking?" Jamal asked as he pulled out of the parking lot to his apartment complex.

"Yeah," Maurice hesitated.

"Mar, what aren't you telling me?"

Maurice whispered. "Look, this really isn't a conversation for the phone, you know what I mean? All I'ma say is Keisha is positive that Samir had something to do with having Kiree taken out."

"Then she needs to keep her mouth closed because history shows Samir is not bias when it comes to taking out women."

"Don't you think I know that? Look can you get to Philly tonight?" Maurice asked.

"I have to work tonight," Jamal replied.

"Damn… well look if you can get to Philly soon, let me know. It's more but I can't talk on the phone. I'm in the hospital and there are security guards nearby."

"I'll see what I can do. I'm about to head in. I'ma hit you back. Give my condolences to Keisha and Ms. Becky,"

Maurice hesitated again. "We just got word that Ms. Becky passed away. After they told her what happened to Kiree and Manny, she had a heart attack. She passed like an hour ago."

Jamal let out a loud sigh and shook his head. "Damn… Ms. Becky used to babysit me and Shawn when we were kids. I'ma talk to my Lieutenant. I'll tell her I had a death in the family and I'll be there in about an hour. What hospital are y'all in?"

"You know it's always the same one."

"Temple…" they said at the same time.

"Alright, I'll be there." Jamal disconnected the call as he pulled into the parking lot of the station. He went inside and made his way over to his desk.

"Williams, in my office now," the Lieutenant called down to Jamal.

Jamal sat his things on his desk and made his way over to her office.

"Close the door and have a seat," she said as she took her glasses off and leaned on her desk.

Lieutenant Armstrong was a short Italian woman with striking features; long black curly hair that she mostly kept either in a ponytail or in a bun. She wore eye glasses that she sometimes tilted off of her nose as she looked over the rim of them at whomever she was speaking to. She was a woman who commanded respect by her presence alone and never took bull-shit from anyone.

"How are you, Lou?" Jamal asked with a sly grin. He knew she hated when he called her that.

"Detective Davidson called again. He wanted to inform you that your Aunt Rebecca Stephens passed away from a heart attack. Apparently, her son Kiree Stephens was killed in a shooting and his brother Emmanuel is fighting for his life. He wanted to know how soon you could make it to Philly?"

Jamal's face was blank. Though Ms. Becky was close to him as a kid growing up, she wasn't his aunt and Kiree and Manny weren't his cousins. He was curious as to why the detective would lie to get him to come to Philly. He didn't like the sound of this.

Jamal cleared his throat. "I um… I'm not sure. I'm on duty tonight and I have some paper work to finish up."

"Take some time off and go be with your family," the Lieutenant suggested. "That's got to be difficult to deal with."

"I had just gotten the news before I got here. I figured I would go tomorrow before work."

"No, go be with your family tonight. You rarely ever take any time off. One thing I admire about you is that you're very dedicated. So take this week off and go be with your family. Make sure everything and everybody is okay. That's an order."

Jamal sat quietly before he made his way to the door. "Thanks Lou," he said with his back turned to her. He left the precinct and went to sit in his car. He looked in his phone at Davidson's number for a moment before finally pressing the call button. His heart pounded in his chest while he patiently awaited an answer.

"Davidson," a voice responded on the other end of the line.

"This is Detective Jamal Williams returning your phone call. You told my Lieutenant that my aunt and cousin passed away. Ms. Becky wasn't my aunt and

Kiree wasn't my cousin. Who are you and what do you want?" Jamal asked suspiciously.

"I need you in Philly to discuss something in regards to a case that I'm working on," Davidson replied, happy to have finally gotten a hold of Jamal.

"And I'm sure you know I wouldn't be able to help you with any case because that district is out of my jurisdiction."

"Trust me; you can help more than you think. I just want a fresh perspective from someone who is from the area, who's been in the streets and knows the people." Davidson paused hoping that Jamal was buying what he was selling.

Jamal was still suspicious but curiosity was nagging him. He knew it was more to it than what the cop was saying. "I'll call when I get to Philly." He disconnected the call before Davidson could respond. Jamal leaned back on the head rest of his car seat thinking. He reached for Tamera's ring that hung around his neck again and played with it between his fingers while getting a nagging feeling in the pit of his stomach. He kissed the ring and let it fall back against his chest. Then, against his better judgment, he started his car and made his way back to Philly.

5

Samir stood in his office leaning on his cherry wood desk. He held a handful of darts and threw one after another as he thought to himself. All he needed was for Manny and Kiree to be out of the way and he could claim Blumberg Projects along with the surrounding blocks. He was strong arming the guys in that area with no mercy. Either you worked for him or you got worked over. There was no room for negotiation. His phone went off.

"Yo!" Samir answered on his blue tooth as he threw another dart, aiming for the bullzeye.

"Sa' we got a problem yo," the man on the other end of the phone replied.

"A problem like what, Chris? Why are you calling me? Where are Mark and Rob?"

"They're dead, man. They got cancelled."

Samir slammed the darts onto his desk. "Fuck you mean they got cancelled? Are you telling me their punk asses couldn't take out two lousy hits?" Samir was furious.

"They cancelled Kiree," Chris replied nervously.

"What about Manny?" Samir asked.

"I heard he was in Temple, critical."

"So who the fuck took them out? Was somebody else out there with them?"

"I think so."

"You find out who and you find out now!" Samir yelled into the phone. With Manny alive and another gunman on the loose, retaliation would be soon to follow if he didn't act fast.

"It doesn't take a genius to know who else was with them, Sa'. We think it was D-Ball," Chris replied.

"You find that punk bitch and rock his ass to sleep A-fucking SAP," Samir growled.

"We're already on it. I was with one of my guys up at the hospital. I saw Manny's girl there talking to her brother. I heard him make a phone call," Chris trailed off.

"To who?" Samir asked.

"To Jamal, I think."

Samir laughed and threw another dart. "That pussy-ass Toy Cop can't do shit. He ain't been right since his girl got murked. He's a non-fucking-factor. Keep an eye on Keisha and Maurice. And when you find D-Ball's ass, bring him to me. I've been wanting to get him the fuck outta here for a long time. His time is up." He disconnected the call. Samir began to wonder why Maurice reached out to Jamal. What could he possibly do? He dismissed his thoughts and figured just as he said to his minion; Jamal is a non-factor. But something about Jamal's presence in the city bothered him. He thought again that maybe he shouldn't dismiss his cousin's return to Philly.

6

Keisha was sitting in Manny's hospital room listening to the doctors as they explained his injuries. Luckily no serious damage was done and Manny was expected to make a slow recovery. The doctors explained if the bullets had been two inches closer to the left, they would have taken out his heart and Manny would have been a goner. Keisha put her hands to her face and wept, partly in relief and partly in sorrow because Manny's brother and mother had been lost due to the senseless violence. She thanked sweet Jesus that he spared her son's father and the love of her life. Changes were going to be made once Manny recuperated. There was no way she could handle this type of devastation again. Both she and the doctors agreed that it would be best if the news of his mother's death were kept from him until he was stronger. They left Keisha alone in the room with him. She pulled a chair over to Manny's bed side and sat next to him so she could hold his hand. She closed her eyes and spoke softly as the tears continued to fall.

"I love you so much. I don't know what I would do without you." She felt him squeeze her hand and opened her eyes. He didn't need to say anything. She knew he was telling her that he loved her too just by the way he was looking at her. He let go of her hand and made a motion as best as he could. It looked as though he was trying to write something.

"You want a pen and paper?" Keisha asked. Manny grunted and nodded his head. She looked around and spotted a tablet and a pen on a table nearby. She grabbed it and gave it to him. Manny struggled to write and was only able to get out two letters.

"K I," Keisha said as she looked at the paper. "K I? You want Kamir?" she asked him. Manny grunted again and shook his head. He then crossed his middle finger over his pointer finger and tapped the bed. Keisha looked at him confused and then looked at the paper. "Kiree...?" she asked as she looked at Manny. Manny nodded his head. Keisha looked at Manny and then looked at the floor. She opened her mouth to speak but the words wouldn't come. Manny searched her face and knew the situation wasn't good. He grabbed the sheets and closed his eyes groaning. Keisha could hear him saying no repeatedly. She knelt beside him trying to calm him down. "I know baby, I know.

I'm sorry. I'm so sorry. But I need you to calm down and stay strong. You've gotta be strong for Kiree, and for Kamir and for me. We need you to get better. Please…" Keisha begged.

Manny breathed heavy and looked at her. Keisha could clearly see murder in his eyes. He made the hand motion for the pen and paper again. Keisha gave it to him. His hand shook as he struggled to write the word "Key". He then wrote out a series of numbers: 5, 24, 10, 26. Keisha looked at the numbers, confused. "My birthday and your birthday? I don't understand." She looked at the word *key* and then looked at the numbers. "The *key*?" Keisha asked.

Manny nodded his head. It then became clear.

Outside of Manny's brother Kiree, Keisha was the only one who knew where Manny kept his money. In the floor of their bedroom was a safe that Manny kept his money in along with two guns. He explained to Keisha that if anything were to happen to him, she was to *use the key*, take their son and get the hell out of dodge immediately. Today was that day.

"No Manny, I'm not leaving you. We're in this together no matter what. You're stuck with me, you understand?" Keisha said with tears in her eyes.

Manny hit the bed as hard as he could. He was dead serious. He suspected something was about to go down for a while but hoped that he made it out with Keisha and their son before the shit hit the fan. He grabbed her hand and squeezed it. "I love you," he struggled to say. "You gotta go, now."

Maurice came into the room. He looked at Manny and nodded. Manny stared at him momentarily and then looked back at Keisha. He pushed the paper into her hand and she made a fist around it. Their eyes locked and she nodded her head knowing exactly what she needed to do. She walked over to her brother.

"We've gotta go now," she said to him.

"Go where?" Maurice asked.

"I can't explain right now. Is your car here?" Keisha asked as they walked out of the room.

"Yeah, it is." Before Maurice could ask another question, Keisha flagged down Angela.

"Grab Kamir, let's go," she instructed.

"Wait, don't you want to stay here with Manny?" Angela asked confused.

"Look, I need both of y'all to stop asking me questions and just come the fuck on," Keisha said through her teeth with fire in her eyes. She looked from her brother to Angela and then made her way over to the elevator. Neither of them noticed the guy in a chair pretending to read a newspaper. He was one of Samir's men sent to watch them. He had just gotten the call from Samir to kill them all.

They jumped on the elevator and rode down to the garage. Neither Maurice nor Angela knew what to say to Keisha so they followed in silence. They made their way over to Maurice's Dodge Charger and jumped inside. They were pulling out just as two of Samir's men were coming into the garage.

"We just missed them," one said to Samir on the phone.

"Follow them. And this time don't fuck up," Samir instructed.

They ran to their car and jumped in, following behind Maurice and Keisha.

Maurice's cell phone rang. It was Jamal. "Yo!" he answered.

"Yo, I just got off 95. I'm on my way down the way," Jamal told him.

"Is that Jamal?" Keisha asked.

"Yeah, hold on." Maurice said to his sister.

"No, tell Jamal to meet us at my apartment ASAP," Keisha said. She rattled off the address and Maurice repeated it to Jamal.

"Alright, I'll meet y'all there," Jamal said before disconnecting the call.

"Enough of this 007 shit, Keisha. What the fuck is going on? You better tell me and you better tell me now," Maurice demanded.

Keisha took a deep breath. "Manny told me to *use the key*." Keisha replied.

"Okay… am I supposed to know what that means?" Maurice asked sarcastically.

"Manny planned for this day but he hoped it never came. I need to get something from the apartment and bounce tonight. Manny doesn't think it's over."

They drove to her apartment and hopped on the elevator. When they got to her floor and made their way down the hall, Keisha spotted D-Ball standing by her apartment door.

"What the hell are you doing here?" Keisha seethed as she marched over to him.

"Wait, Keisha. Before you go off on me, let me explain. I just wanted you to know I ain't leave Manny and Kiree hanging. I took them niggas out and then I had to go because the cops were coming. I only came by to give you something. Manny told me if anything were to happen to him, to tell you to use the key." He reached into his pocket and put a piece of paper in her hand that had the same numbers written on them.

Keisha looked down at the paper that he placed in her hand. She frowned and shook her head as the tears came. "He's still alive," she said as she looked up at him.

D-Ball nodded his head. "I know. I called the hospital to find out." Keisha unlocked the door and they all went inside. She instructed Angela to take her son in his bedroom and grab some of his clothes.

"They're going to be coming for me next so I can't stay long. I made a promise to Manny…" he trailed off and shook his head. "I told Kiree that Samir was setting us up," he said angrily.

"So it was Samir," Keisha concluded as she went inside of the floor where the safe was hidden.

"Fuck yeah it was him. That nigga wants Blumberg so bad. He's strong arming all those niggas around there but he wasn't trying to go up against us. We wasn't trying to hear that shit. Fuck that nigga," D-Ball replied. Maurice watched his sister as she pulled a gun from the safe and slammed a clip into it and checked to see if a round was chambered. Keisha caught the way he was looking at her.

Keisha sighed deeply. "Manny always wanted me to protect myself. He said: A girl can't be too safe in these crime ridden times. After I got pregnant with Kamir, he made sure I got my license to carry and took me to the gun range on a regular." Keisha explained as she loaded the second gun.

Maurice shook his head. "This shit is unreal…"

"No this shit just got real," Keisha replied as she threw the money in a duffle bag. She took out an envelope and opened it. Inside was a copy of a lease to a house in Glenolden with a set of keys. She tucked everything back in the envelope and put it in her purse. She looked around at the apartment they shared for almost four years. The memories of all the love and happy moments made in their home flooded her mind. She shook her head as she fought back the tears. Maurice grabbed the duffle bag.

"Angie, let's go!" Keisha called out. D-Ball opened the door and stepped out first with Keisha behind him. He looked up the hall and saw the two men dressed in leather jackets, sun glasses and fitted hats. He had a split second to choose between grabbing his gun and pushing Keisha back into the apartment so she didn't get hit. Just as the first guy fired, he practically closed lined Keisha back into the apartment but not fast enough before a bullet caught him in his thigh. Keisha screamed. Maurice tried closing the door but D-Ball was caught in the doorway.

"Move! Move!" D-Ball screamed at Maurice. He pulled both of his guns from his waist and fired out of the door causing the gunmen to jump back and giving D-Ball enough time to scoot inside of the apartment. Maurice slammed and locked the door.

"Get my son outta here!" Keisha screamed to Angela. Little Kamir was screaming and crying once he saw his Uncle D bleeding from his leg. They made their way to the back bedroom. Keisha closed their bedroom door. She then opened the bathroom window and closed the bathroom door. Lastly she closed the back bedroom door where they all were hiding.

"Take my son down the fire escape Angie, now! Get him out of here now!" Keisha said to Angie.

"What about you?" Angie said as she backed up to the window.

"I'll be fine. Take D-Ball with you." Keisha said.

"Fuck that, Keisha! You go with Angie and me and D-Ball will stay," Maurice said as he snatched one of the guns from his sister.

"D-Ball is already hit and I'm not leaving you," Keisha said to her brother. She looked at D-Ball. "Thank you."

"Don't mention it," D-Ball groaned as he hobbled to the window. They heard a shot outside of the apartment where someone was shooting one of the locks off. Keisha prayed like hell one of the neighbors called the cops. But she knew the chances of them getting there in time were slim to none. Angie helped Kamir out of the window. He cried for his mommy. Keisha told him she loved him. D-Ball was the last one out of the window and they made their way down the fire escape.

"I hope you know how to use that," Keisha said to her brother as she slid over to one of the walk-in closets in the room. The two were in a great position to get the drop on an ambush before an ambush happened; one was behind the bedroom door and the other was across from it. Thankfully it was dark so you couldn't tell when coming in the bedroom if the closet door was opened or closed.

"Remember that game on the 8 bit Nintendo we used to play; Duck Hunt?" Maurice replied. He made his way over to the other closet. "Well, those niggas are the ducks. And I'm the muthafucking hunter." He backed inside of the closet and aimed at the bedroom door. Keisha backed into the other closet and crouched down also aiming at the door.

They heard when the gunmen entered the apartment. Keisha could hear her heart beating in her ears. Maurice kept his eyes on the door and said a prayer to himself. They heard when the gunmen kicked in the first bedroom door and then the bathroom. The door knob to the bedroom they were in turned and then opened slowly. Keisha thanked Manny for not putting the light bulbs in the ceiling fan like she asked him to for the last week. The first guy felt along the wall for the light switch and flicked it. When nothing happened, he eased into the room. The light from the bathroom allowed Keisha to see him but he still could not see them. She aimed her gun and squeezed the trigger twice. The first bullet spun him around and the second bullet hit him in the chest, knocking him down. Maurice stayed put knowing that there was another gunman. Hearing the first two shots, the second gunman shot wildly into the room in Maurice's direction. Maurice took a hit and fell inside of the closet. Keisha screamed for her brother. She heard three more shots and then it was quiet.

Jamal pushed the door in aiming his gun at the gunman on the floor not moving. He kicked him.

"Maurice! Keisha!" Jamal called out.

Yani

Keisha scrambled from the closet. She turned a lamp on and then ran over to the closet that Maurice was in. Maurice was still alive but unconscious after taking a bullet in his side. Keisha cried hysterically.

"Keisha!" Jamal yelled. "He's alive, but the cops are on their way. You need to do something with this money before they get here. Are there any drugs in here?" Jamal asked her.

"No, Manny never brought his work home," Keisha said. She was getting dizzy. Today was too much for her to handle. She couldn't believe she just killed a man! She needed to sit down.

Jamal grabbed her by her shoulders and shook her to snap her back to reality and get her to understand she had mere minutes to make a move. "Keisha, listen to me. You need to do something with that money and now!"

Keisha scrambled back to her bedroom and moved the bed. She pulled the floor up and opened the safe. She threw the money back inside, locked the safe and put the floor back as it was with the bed over top. She tossed the duffle bag back inside of the closet and then went back to her brother. Jamal placed a pillow under his head and put a blanket over him as he called it in. He then grabbed a towel and told Keisha to apply pressure to Maurice's wound.

Two white cops were the first ones on the scene. "Hands on your head!" They shouted to Jamal when they saw him standing in the doorway of the apartment.

Jamal looked at them confused. "Wait…" he tried to say.

One of the cops moved closer to him aiming his gun. "Put your hands on your head where I can see them and move against the wall!" Jamal did as he was told and shook his head.

"You got any weapons on you or any sharp objects that might stick me?" the cop asked as he put his gun in his holster. "What the fuck are you doing up here anyway, huh?" he asked in a smug tone.

Jamal shook his head as he spread his legs so he could be searched. "Yeah, I do. I have my gun and I have my fucking badge, bitch. I'm a detective with the Wilmington DE Police Department."

The officer patted him down. He took his gun and then found his badge on his waist. The other cop came behind him.

"Is that legit?" the second cop asked.

"I dunno. Call it in and find out. Until then, you sit your ass against that wall," the first cop said smugly.

"Man, while the two of you are busy jerking your dicks, my best friend is in there bleeding to death with his sister. It's fucking ridiculous how you see a brother in a white apartment complex and automatically assume he's a fucking criminal," Jamal snapped.

"Spare me the racial speech, Obama," the cop said. Jamal shook his head.

Moments later the ambulance came down the hallway. They made their way inside of the apartment so they could help Maurice. Soon more cops followed and neighbors began coming out of their apartments wanting to know what happened.

As they wheeled Maurice out on the stretcher, Keisha was right by his side. She saw Jamal on the floor.

"What the hell are y'all doing?! He just saved my life and my brother's life! He's a detective, what the hell are y'all doing?!" she asked hysterically.

"Keisha, go be with your brother, I got this." Jamal told her.

"Ma'am, we need to ask you some questions about what happened here," one of the cops that were holding Jamal said to Keisha as he grabbed her arm.

"Get your fucking hands off of me. I've already answered their questions. I'm going to be with my brother. If y'all want to talk to me some more, contact my lawyer," Keisha hissed as she snatched away from the officer. She ran down the hall to catch up with the medics and Maurice.

"Hey," the first cop said. "He checks out. Detective Jamal Williams with the DPD." He tossed Jamal his badge. "Sorry about that. It's just with the madness going on, we just couldn't be sure."

Jamal stood up and snatched his gun when it was held out to him. "Whatever."

"This is way out of your jurisdiction. What are you doing here, anyway?" the second cop asked.

Jamal tucked his gun in the back of his pants. "The young lady that just left is the girlfriend of the man who rents this apartment. He was shot earlier and his brother was killed. They're family of mine. I was coming from D-E when she asked me if I could meet her here. As I'm coming off the elevator, I heard gunshots. When I got down here, I saw blood on the floor and in the doorway and the lock was shot off. I heard more gunshots from inside of the apartment. I came in and did what I had to do," Jamal explained.

"Is this some kind of drug thing?" the cop asked.

Yani

Jamal looked at him for a brief moment and then shrugged. "This is out of my jurisdiction, remember? You tell me."

7

Detective Davidson sat at his desk leaned back in his chair with his hands clasped behind his head. His eyes were closed as he rocked in his chair in deep thought. Jamal was his key to taking down Samir. He just needed a way to persuade Jamal to get on his team. There wasn't much that he could go on so he knew he had to do some digging into Jamal's past for information on him such as who his parents were and how deep his connection with Samir was outside of them just being family. He was waiting for some information to come back on Jamal's file. Though it was expunged, it could still be obtained.

"Davidson," a voice said from behind. Keith looked up and saw a female officer holding a folder out to him. "This is everything we have on Jamal Williams."

Davidson sat up eagerly and took the file. "How far back does it go?" he asked as he began flipping through it.

"It goes back to July 1998. He was brought in for questioning in regards to the murder of Khalil Dixon. It looks like there was nothing concrete so they let him go. The case was later closed and left unsolved," the cop explained.

Davidson looked at the file. "I remember when that happened. Allegedly, Khalil shot and killed a young man a week before that."

"Yes, that's in there as well. Jamal was to be questioned for that murder also, but when Khalil was murdered, Jamal was let go for that too," she further explained as she sat on the edge of the desk.

"Heh," Davidson snorted with a smirk on his face. "How convenient. Look at this shit; petty drug charges, fighting, aggravated assault, misdemeanors, accessory… none of this shit stuck?" Davidson asked as he looked up at the officer.

She shrugged. "From what I can see."

"I need a record of every arresting officer for Jamal. I want to know who processed his paper work for every release. Is that in the file?" he asked.

"Yeah, everything is in there. It looks like two of the same officers were the ones who processed him; umm, Johnson and Parker. Parker was killed in a shoot-out in the Olney section back in 2010 and his partner Johnson was the cop who was killed in that botched home invasion a few months back. No suspects, no arrests."

Davidson stared at the file. *"Isn't that convenient?"* he mused. There was a connection and he didn't have long to figure it out. "Are there any cops alive that processed Jamal, arrested him, questioned him, whatever?"

"I didn't read through the entire file so I don't know," the female cop responded. "Why are you digging into this guy's past?"

"I had a hunch," Davidson mumbled. He let out a deep sigh and tossed the folder onto his desk. "Thanks."

"No problem," she replied as she left his desk.

Davidson leaned back in his chair and closed his eyes. He was drifting into deep thought again when his phone rang. "Davidson," he replied without looking at the caller ID.

"This is Jamal. Manny's girlfriend and her brother were just ambushed at her apartment. Her brother was shot and is in the hospital," Jamal said. Davidson sat straight up in his chair. "You've got to be kidding me."

"No, I'm not. And it gets worse. They just handcuffed Keisha and took her to the police station."

"For what?" Davidson asked.

Jamal was silent for a moment. "She killed one of the gunmen."

"WHAT!?" Davidson barked.

"Look, there's no time for me to explain. You said you wanted to see me. I'm on my way to Temple Hospital to see Manny and Dante Smith."

"D-Ball?" Davidson asked, familiar with the name. "What is he doing there?"

"You don't really think I'm going to continue this conversation over the phone, do you? Meet me at Temple Hospital. You have ten minutes to convince me why I should help you with this so called case and then I'm on the first thing back to Delaware. Whatever the fuck is going on down here, I don't want no part of it." Jamal disconnected the call.

Davidson bolted from his chair and snatched up his jacket. He hurried out of the precinct and made his way over to Temple University Hospital.

Jamal entered the hospital and showed his badge to the receptionist. "My name is Detective Jamal Williams. Could you tell me where I can find Dante Smith?"

The receptionist checked the computer log. "He's in room 505 in stable condition."

"Thanks," Jamal replied before making his way over to the elevator. He hadn't seen D-Ball since Tamera's funeral. He was nervous about seeing his old friend under these circumstances. He took a deep breath before knocking on the door.

"Come in," D-Ball said. He was lying in the bed with his leg elevated. He had an arm over his face with his eyes closed. So much had happened in a matter of a few hours. He watched his best friend get murdered, his other friend was worse off than he was and he barely survived another ambush. He made it up in his mind right then and there that he was finished and the minute he was released from the hospital, he was getting as far away from Philly as possible and leaving the street life alone.

"D-Ball," Jamal said, snapping him out of his thoughts.

D-Ball looked up at Jamal, shocked. "What are you doing here?"

"Maurice called me. Keisha wanted me to find you before Samir did."

"Yeah, well we just got ambushed by those pussies again." He looked at Jamal. "Is she okay? Is her son and Maurice okay?"

"They're fine. I got there just in time," Jamal said as he pulled up a chair. "Maurice got hit and Keisha…" Jamal trailed off.

"What? Keisha what? I thought you said they were okay." D-Ball said. His heart was racing.

Jamal shook his head. "Keisha popped one of them."

D-Ball smiled. "Yeah, fuck them niggas. They ain't realize Keisha is a fucking rider. We trained her well."

"What do you mean?" Jamal asked.

D-Ball looked at Jamal and shook his head. "Man, you're a whole pig now," he said with a look of disgust on his face. "After everything we've been through growing up; the way them niggas hide behind their badges and will beat a brown nigga down like you and me as if we ain't one of the same and you on their side now?" D-Ball hissed.

"It's not like that," Jamal started.

"Then what the fuck is it? Man, I know what happened to your girl and your daughter was fucked up, but you bailed on some bitch shit. We told you we had your back. We were in a position to take Samir out when that shit went down with those fucking Columbians. But you bounced." D-Ball shook his head. "Man, I ain't got shit to say to you."

Jamal stared at his friend for a moment. "Are you done? Let's get something straight. When those muthafuckas killed my girl while she was pregnant with my daughter, I had no reason to stay. What the fuck for? I could've killed Samir without a second thought, too. But I was tired of that shit. That's the fuck why I was caught up in the bullshit in the first place; trying to get revenge."

"Do you know how much of a difference it would've made if somebody had put Samir down a long fucking time ago? Kiree would still be alive. Manny would be home playing the Wii with his son. Keisha would be cooking dinner. Ms. Becky would be doing her thing. But look at what the fuck is happening instead. Look how many lives were destroyed because this nigga is so fucking power hungry."

Jamal shook his head. "We don't know that. There's always a nigga in line waiting to take over. Look D-Ball, I didn't come here as a cop. I came as a friend. What we talk about in here is between me and you. You got my word on that," Jamal assured him.

D-Ball looked at him feeling unsure. "What do you know and what do you want to know?" he asked.

"I don't know much. I didn't get a chance to talk to Keisha before y'all were ambushed. Now they have her at a police station. I can't do much because this ain't my area. But I can tell you this: Samir wants you dead. And whatever is going on made Keisha and Maurice a target, too. I wouldn't be surprised if they'd kill Kamir just in case. What the fuck is going on down here?"

D-Ball sat quiet for a moment. Though he wasn't a snitch, too much had happened today and too many lives were at stake. Something had to be done. He began explaining to Jamal how the pieces began moving like a chess game in 2002 when the Columbians began using Samir to move their shipments into the neighborhoods. Little by little, parts of Samir's territory was being taken, his power was diminishing. It made room for a new group of drug dealers to make more money than they were making with Samir having control of so many territories. Most of the guys who feared Samir were only afraid because of the police force he had backing him. With the Columbians muscling in on his territory, slowly but surely Samir would lose that backing and could be taken out.

"That's one of the reasons we were so pissed when you rolled, Jamal. We knew if anybody could get close enough to Samir to take him out, it would have been you.

"When the Columbians took over Blumberg, a lot of Samir's soldiers were getting booked. Some of them were getting hit with charges that not even Samir could help them beat. Shit got real crazy when this Detective

Kristoff got killed on his way to his car one night. From what I heard, somebody walked up behind him and slit his throat," D-Ball explained.

Jamal's heart started racing as he stared at D-Ball. "Kristoff?" he asked. "You said his name was Kristoff?"

"Yeah, why?" D-Ball asked back.

"Are you sure he was a cop?"

"Yeah; Alekzander Kristoff. Now and again he would pop up in the neighborhood…"

Jamal interrupted him, "That can't be. He couldn't have been a cop." Jamal began thinking back to the story that his mother told him about how his father was killed. He remembered his mother speaking on a man named Kristoff, saying he was a rival of his father's and a man named Smitty. She never mentioned what happened with Kristoff after Samir killed his father. He assumed that he was either in jail or dead.

"Why does it matter?" D-Ball asked as he noticed the serious yet confused look on Jamal's face. "Did you know him?"

"No…" Jamal said as his thoughts continued to wander. "What happened after Kristoff was killed?"

"Samir started going hard as hell. Every time you turned around, niggas was getting murked up Girard

Avenue, Johnson Homes, Master Street and Thompson Street. It's like he was sending a message: If you wanted to work and live to count your paper, you worked for him and no one else." D-Ball continued.

"Yeah; but how could he just do that with the Columbians pulling the strings?" Jamal asked.

"Rumor has it that Samir put the hit out on Kristoff because he was behind the Columbians bringing their shipments in on his territory. They were cutting Kristoff a bigger piece of the pie and it was only a matter of time before he took Samir out. So a lot of niggas think Samir beat him to the punch. Next thing you know, little by little, Samir started getting control of certain areas back. People were coming up missing. A couple of cops were getting murked. That cop that got killed up Olney last year was one of them. His partner set him up."

"This shit is crazy," Jamal said in a low voice as he rubbed his hands over his face.

"You don't know the half of it. It's so many dirty cops on the force; except now, it's hard to tell who's working for Samir and who's working for the Columbians."

"So how did you, Kiree and Manny get on Samir's bad side? What made y'all a target?"

D-Ball was quiet for a moment. "The cop that was killed up Olney, Parker; he came to us in '08 and struck a deal with Kiree to work with the Columbians. It was cool because Kiree's connect got murked out in New York and things were getting crazy. We weren't even trying to work for Samir's bitch-ass. So Kiree and Manny were like, cool. We got the Columbian connect, shit was flowing, everything was all good. We kept Blumberg popping; no beef, no drama. But Parker's partner Johnson was on Samir's team and found out what was going on. Next thing you know, he gets killed in some bull-shit shooting up Olney. But Kiree said fuck that and set up a meeting with the Columbians himself to keep shit moving. Samir tried to move on us a couple times with his little bitch-ass niggas but we wasn't trying to hear that. Then all of a sudden, last summer he wanted a truce. Kiree bought that shit but me and Manny were like naw, Samir setting us up. Manny wanted out because he knew shit was about to get crazy. That's why we started taking Keisha to the gun-range." D-Ball looked at Jamal. "He said he remembered what happened to Tammy and to this day he swears Samir was behind that shit. And he said he wasn't about to let the same shit happen to Keisha and their son."

Jamal looked away. The pain of what happened to Tamera and their unborn child was visible in his face. No matter how well he thought he planned things out, he never factored in the possibility of teaching Tamera how to use a gun for her own protection. What a difference that could have made. He thought that he would always be there to protect her. He was thinking at that point that he was wrong.

Jamal cleared his throat. "So that's why they came after y'all today. Samir figured if he took Manny and Kiree out, the demand for a connection would need to be filled and it would be easier for him to step in and claim Blumberg along with those surrounding blocks," he concluded.

"Pretty much," D-Ball agreed.

Jamal shook his head. "Samir didn't factor in the possibility that you would be there."

"Yeah, and his bitch-ass should've known I rides for mine point fucking blank. And if he wasn't such a pussy and actually took care of shit himself, I'dda killed his ass a long muthafucking time ago," D-Ball seethed. He trembled with fury.

A knock came at the door and then Davidson peeped in. D-Ball looked at Jamal and then looked at Davidson. "What is he doing here?" he asked.

"His business is with me, not you, D-Ball." Jamal told him.

"Actually, my business is with both of you," Davidson said back. He closed the door behind him. "Dante, I need to ask you some questions about the shooting on 24th & Oxford."

"Do we have to do this now?" Jamal asked as he stood up.

"Listen, he can either do this with me, or he can do this with some random cop, take a chance on going out on the streets and having someone finish what was started today. Now it's your choice." Davidson looked at D-Ball with seriousness in his face. He then looked at Jamal. Jamal was trying hard to read his expression but couldn't. He thought over what Davidson said and then had his own thought. He leaned over and whispered in D-Ball's ear

"He's trying to avoid you talking to a cop on Samir's team and having the wrong info get back to him."

"Fuck that, I got nothing to say," D-Ball said, defiantly.

"D-Ball…" Davidson and Jamal said at the same time.

"D-Ball, listen to me. The streets are talking. And they are placing you at the shooting and claiming you took out the two gunmen. Now, you can take your chances and plea self-defense, try to come up with a bull-shit alibi, you can even try to run. But you need to factor in that not only will Samir be looking for you, but so will the cops. And not all of those cops are on the right side of the law," Davidson explained.

"He's right," Jamal said as he looked at Davidson. "How do you know about the cops?" he asked suspiciously.

Davidson lowered his voice. "I have the unfortunate duty of being the one on the scene for the majority of these shootings and have noticed a few things; which is what I need to talk to you about, Jamal."

"You've been real cryptic since the first time we've spoken. What the hell do I have to do with anything and I haven't been in this city in more than nine years?" Jamal asked.

"I'll get to that," Davidson replied. He then looked at D-Ball. "I've bought you some time, but not much. I've set up an alibi that places you in Jenkintown today house-sitting. I have a friend who will swear to that. Since you were shot in that area today, now it appears that you couldn't have been in North Philly when Kiree was murdered. Now, that will get the cops off your ass but I doubt Samir will fall for it."

"Why are you bent on helping me? I ain't nothing but another nigga from the 'hood." D-Ball asked as he looked at Davidson. He was trying to figure out the cop's angle.

"Kiree was a good friend of mine. And so was Manny. You weren't able to save Kiree, but I wholeheartedly believe you saved Manny. In your eyes you might just be another nigga from the 'hood, but to their family, to Keisha, to their son; you're a hero," Davidson replied.

Jamal stood and shook D-Ball's hand, "I'll be back to check in on you. Let me know if you need anything." He grabbed a piece of paper and took a pen from his jacket pocket before scribbling his number down. He then left behind Detective Davidson.

"We need to talk Jamal," Davidson said.

"Yeah, you've been saying that since you first contacted me. But so far you haven't said shit. What exactly is it that you need to talk about?"

Davidson stared at Jamal for a moment as fear knotted his stomach. "Khalil, Raheem and July of '98."

8

Deisha had come home from a long day at the office. One of her patients, a 15 year old girl with extreme anger issues, had finally opened up about being molested by her step-father. She confided in Deisha about her thoughts of suicide and her thoughts of killing her abuser. It broke Deisha's heart to listen to the young lady pour her heart out through constant sobs, but what broke her heart even more was when she was forced to have the young lady committed to avoid having her harm herself as well as anyone else.

Though she had to abide by the confidentiality clause in her practice, she was pondering excessively on how she could convince her patient to file a complaint against the step-father so the sick bastard could be put away.

She had made a life for herself as a Child Psychiatrist with Thomas Jefferson Hospital. Since she worked in Center City, she leased a luxurious condo not too far from her practice so she could walk to and from the office. Keisha didn't work too far from her and sometimes they would have lunch together. But since picking up this last client along with the extra time that she was giving to her at no extra charge, she didn't have time in almost a month to meet with her friend.

Deisha stepped inside of her snug and cozy condo. It was furnished completely by Raymour and Flanigan with a chocolate colored Alexander Leather sofa, a matching love seat and ottoman in her living room. African patterned rugs covered her living room floor and Tuscan striped, thermal patterned curtains adorned her floor to ceiling windows which over looked the skyline of Center City. African paintings hung on her walls along with her favorite enlarged photos of Malcolm X, Martin Luther King Jr. and President Barack Obama. African sculptures and miniature figurines lined her shelves and she had a floor to ceiling book-case that mostly held a variety of literature by her favorite African-American authors.

She took her heels off and placed them inside of her closet along with her coat and suit jacket. As she rotated her neck, she made her way over to her refrigerator and pulled out her bottle of Jose Cuervo Margarita, and fixed herself a drink. She pressed the button on her answering machine and let her messages play back. The first was from Chanda: *"Ciao Deisha! Ho chiamato per dire ciao e per lasciare che tu mi conosci, Shawn ed i bambini vogliono vederti stasera Skype. Ci manchi, ragazza! Ti amo a pezzi!"* Deisha laughed out loud. She loved that Chanda was enjoying her life over in Italy with Shawn while he played basketball overseas, but she had told her so many times not to leave messages in Italian. The only part that she caught was "Skype". They were due for a session and she missed her god-children terribly.

Deisha sipped her drink as she looked up at her high-school graduation picture that she had enlarged and framed of herself, Shawn, Jamal, Maurice, Chanda and Tamera.

"Tammy... I wonder how things would be if you were still here. I miss you..." Deisha said to herself. She felt her eyes begin to sting from the tears that threatened to fall and blinked them away. She stopped the answering machine not wanting to hear the rest of the messages and sat down with her Macbook. She immediately got on Facebook to see what was happening. She damn near spit out her drink as she scrolled through her news feed.

"RIP Kiree..." she read aloud. "WHAT!!!!" She hurriedly jumped to her friends' list and searched for Kiree's name. "No, no, no, no... please God, no... please," Deisha prayed. Her heart raced as she waited patiently for his page to load. Post after post read "RIP Kiree, Rest in Paradise, Peace in Paradise Prince, PIP cousin." Deisha's heart sank into her stomach. She went back to her friends' list and clicked on Keisha's profile. She couldn't believe what she was reading: *"Free my bitch, Keesh! Punk ass pigs got her knocked on some bullshit. RIP Kiree! Those punk ass pussies better pray Manny make it or it's gonna be a fckn SHIT STORM in North Philly because we ride for ours!!!"*

"What the hell is going on up there???" Deisha asked as her heart raced and her eyes began to tear up. She scrolled past the posts from Keisha's friends who were showing their support and offering their condolences. Finally she saw a post from Keisha:

*"These niggas out here are crazy!! They took my son's uncle and tried to take his dad too! I can't think, I can't breathe all I can do is hope. This shit done gave my mom-n-law a heart attack. Thank God my brother is here... He's always here when I need him. Please God, don't take Manny from me and his son. I don't know what I'll do without him...*tears*."*

Deisha's head was spinning. She put down her drink and thought for a moment. She then logged out of her account and logged into her "dummy" Facebook account. She went to Maurice's page to see if he posted anything about Keisha being arrested and if she had been released. The last post on Keisha's page was around 8:45pm. It was now after 9pm. Deisha froze as she read his page: *"Please keep Maurice, Keisha, and Ms.*

Brown in y'all prayers. My cousin's been shot and is in surgery. It's been a crazy day for my family and we really can use all of the prayers and support that y'all can give. Philly gotta stop the violence yo, seriously!! RIP Kiree!!"

"OH MY GOD!!!" Deisha shrieked before bursting into tears. "Kiree is dead, Manny and Maurice got shot, Keisha is in jail!! What the fuck is going on?" She put her hands to her face sobbing before bolting from the couch and searching frantically for her phonebook. She had Jamal's number somewhere and prayed like hell he didn't change it. She wished that he had a Facebook or Twitter account so she could reach out to him faster. She rummaged through her china cabinet and the drawers before finally coming across her phonebook. Deisha felt like she was two seconds away from screaming as she scanned through the numbers. She yelled in relief when she found Jamal's number and dialed it from her phone with a shaky hand. It rang and she thanked sweet Jesus that it did.

"Hello," a deep voice answered.

"Jamal!!!" Deisha blurted out.

"Yeah, who dis?" Jamal answered.

"It's Deisha. I just saw on Facebook that Kiree is dead, Manny got shot, Maurice got shot..." she broke off as she cried. "I'm sorry for calling like this but... but..." Deisha burst into uncontrollable tears.

"Deisha, calm down," Jamal said. He waited for Deisha to get herself under control. "Where are you?"

"I'm home. But I don't know what hospital Maurice is in or where Keisha is."

"Maurice is at Abington Memorial in Jenkintown, Keisha is being held in Jenkintown. And yea, Kiree was killed, Manny was shot also and Ms. Becky passed from a heart attack after she found out."

"WHAT!!!" Deisha screamed in his ear. "Jamal... what the... I don't understand... I can't... I can't," Deisha said as she paced back and forth in her living room. She sounded as if she were two seconds away from having a panic attack.

"Deisha look, I'm in the middle of something right now."

"Aren't you coming to Philly? Maurice is your best friend!" Deisha said hysterically.

Jamal took a deep breath trying to remain calm. He knew Deisha was upset, but he was upset as well and he didn't want to take it out on her.

"DEISHA! Calm the hell down, okay? Calm down, take a deep breath and chill."

"I can't chill!" Deisha said in tears.

"Listen, I know you and Maurice broke up. But I know he still loves you, and I know you still love him despite how tough you try to act. Give me your address so I can come talk to you. It's a lot going on right now and I need to take care of some things before I come up." Jamal explained.

"You're already in Philly?" Deisha asked.

"Yes, I'm in Philly. What's your address?" Deisha rambled it off to him. "Okay. Let me finish up here and I'll be right over," Jamal disconnected the call and Deisha plopped onto the couch. She placed her hands to her face and sobbed uncontrollably. She had been thinking about Maurice excessively lately and had been back and forth on whether or not she should pick up the phone to call him. Their break up had been entirely her fault. If only she hadn't been so afraid of repeating history and making the same mistakes as her mother. If only she had trusted that Maurice loved her more than anything in the world and would be by her side no matter what. If only she hadn't gotten that abortion. And now something horrible was transpiring. She wanted to make amends with him more than anything in the world. But how...?

9

Jamal sat listening to Detective Davidson for more than an hour. He tried to tell himself that the cop was grasping at straws and there was no way that he could prove his theory. But deep down inside, Jamal knew the cop was on to something.

"You're reaching," Jamal said with a straight face.

"Oh I'm not reaching at all. Now I haven't had a chance to read completely through your file, but just from the little bit that I was able to see, it's not hard to put two and two together," Davidson said with confidence.

"But see the problem with your theory is, you're adding two and two together and getting five. You're way off, cop. And you're wasting my time." Jamal stood up, ready to leave.

"Jamal, I already know that there are cops on the take. Your brother Shawn walked away from a gun beef unscathed. You were supposed to be questioned in a shooting that resulted in a friend of yours being killed. But conveniently, the suspect was killed a few days later. Again you were supposed to be questioned, but mysteriously there was no basis because you had an alibi. It's also convenient that damn near all of the cops that ever arrested you or processed you are dead. Now, no one else has felt the need to look through your file, but do you think they would be so understanding if they did?" Davidson asked quietly.

"I don't care how deep you dig, cop. You've got nothing on me. And you might not want to go sniffing around in shit that's been long buried. Like you said, cops have been turning up dead," Jamal said in a hushed tone.

"Are you threatening me?" Davidson asked.

Jamal leaned onto the desk and looked at him for a moment. "It's not me you have to worry about."

Davidson sat back. "It's not you that I want, Jamal. I want Samir. Come on, after everything you've been through. After watching your best friend get gunned down in front of you, after losing your girlfriend while she was pregnant with your child..."

"You leave her out of this!" Jamal snapped with a look on his face that almost made the detective recoil.

"Nine years later and the mere mention of her fires you up like that yet you refuse to do anything about it."

"What was I supposed to do?! Huh?!" Jamal asked, raising his voice.

"Be a man!" Davidson yelled back as he stood up. "If you didn't have the heart to do anything about it then, do something about it now. Help me stop him."

"I can't help you!" Jamal said loudly causing cops nearby to look at them.

"No you don't *want* to help me." Davidson said in a hushed, harsh tone. They stared daggers at each other.

Jamal began putting his coat on. "I don't know how or why you thought I could help you. I don't know what made you think I *would* help you. If you think you can take on Samir, then do it. But do it without me. My girl..." Jamal hesitated and took a deep breath. "Tammy and my daughter were my only reasons to stay in Philly. They're gone. So am I."

Detective Davidson shook his head as he watched Jamal walk towards the door of his office. "Running won't solve anything. Running doesn't stop the problem. It didn't help when you left nine years ago, it sure as hell won't help this time. Running doesn't make you a man, Jamal. It makes you a punk."

Jamal stopped in his tracks. He wanted to respond but didn't have a response. Instead he shook his head and walked out of the police station and headed straight to Deisha.

10

Keisha sat in a cell alone on top of a cot with her knees to her chest and her arms wrapped around them with her head down. She was terrified at the moment. Her fear wasn't for facing a possible murder charge because she would do it again in a heartbeat to save her brother and her son. But sitting in that jail cell left her with an eerie feeling. She hadn't been allowed to make her phone call and it was almost 10 o'clock at night. She knew her son was worried and she wanted to check on Manny and Maurice. She prayed to God that they were okay and that she was okay as well.

She heard the bars to her cell slide open and looked up. She looked the guy over and could immediately tell that he wasn't her attorney by his police uniform. He appeared not to be the typical beat cop. She was thinking he was more than likely a Sergeant.

"Are you here to take me to make my phone call?" Keisha asked. She was tired and emotionally drained.

"You're being released," the cop said to her. He had a slight grin.

Keisha closed her eyes and leaned her head back against the wall. She mumbled "thank you" before standing up. But when she moved towards the cell doors, the cop stepped in her path. Keisha looked up at him and tried to step around him but he stepped in her path again.

Keisha sighed angrily. "Look, it's late, I'm tired and I need to get home to my son. So can you please stop with the two step so I can go on about my business?"

"You got a lot of sass, girl," the officer said with a creepy smirk on his face. His facial expression unnerved Keisha. She took a step back but the officer reached for her arm and grabbed her. She struggled against him but he was too strong and too powerful. He slammed her into the wall almost knocking the wind out of her and then turned her around with her back facing him. He pinned one arm behind her back to stop her from struggling and pushed her into the wall, smashing her face. Her screams sounded more like muffled grunting. She struggled and squirmed when she felt his hands fondling her breasts before moving between her legs and pushing his fingers against her crotch. Keisha screamed for help as loud as she could.

"I like 'em fiesty like you, bitch," the officer panted as he licked the side of her face and forced his fingers inside of her. "I got a message from Samir for you, bitch," he said as he painfully jammed his fingers in and out of her. "Let this be a warning to you. Next time, we'll send you to your mother's door step in a fucking body bag."

The officer grabbed Keisha by her throat and turned her around. Before she had a chance to brace herself, the cop hauled off and punched her in her face knocking her over the cot and onto the floor. She crawled a few steps before the officer grabbed her by her leg and dragged her back. She kicked frantically but to no avail. The cop forced her over the cot and grabbed her by her throat again. She squealed, scratched and clawed frantically wondering why no one was coming to help her. She could hear the officer panting heavily as well as the sounds of his belt buckle clanking together and she knew what was coming next. She tried with every fiber in her body to fight but he squeezed tighter on her throat as he lift her skirt up and tore her panties off. She felt when he roughly entered her, the pain shooting to her stomach and almost making her vomit. What lasted two minutes felt like an eternity. The cop brutally raped Keisha in the holding cell. Through her tears, sweat and spit, she could smell his Old Spice cologne and his sweat and felt his hot breath on her neck as he panted in excitement in between licking the side of her face like some beastly animal tasting his meal. After pulling out, he tossed Keisha onto the floor of the cell like a rag doll. The throbbing pain between her legs was excruciating and she drew in a breath before letting out a ragged cough that scratched her throat which was sore from screaming and being choked. She closed her eyes and sobbed as she listened to the cop fix his clothing.

"Stand up, bitch," the officer said. As badly as Keisha wanted to, she couldn't move. The cop stood over her and snatched her up by her collar, forcing her to stand. "I said stand up!" He smoothed her hair to the back and made her fix her clothes. He kept her panties, tucking them in his back pocket. "Now, we're going to walk out of here nice and easily, you understand? You say anything and you won't make it out of this precinct breathing. Remember, this was just a warning. Tell your little bitch-ass boyfriend to get the fuck outta dodge. Next time we won't be so nice." He reached out to pat Keisha on the cheek but she flinched. She avoided eye contact. Her face stung from the punch she took and her throat was too sore to speak. She followed the officer to the front so she could be released. Each step she took hurt like hell but she walked as if nothing happened. The female cop that handed Keisha her things looked at her suspiciously. She had a feeling something was wrong.

"Here are your things, Ms. Brown. Do you need an escort?" the female officer asked politely.

Keisha tried to speak but her throat was too sore. She combed her fingers through her hair so that it fell over the side of her face that had been hit. She shook her head avoiding eye contact, collected her things and left.

Once Keisha made it outside of the precinct, she ran. She had no idea which direction she was running in but she ran as fast as she could as she cried. She got to a church and sat on the steps. Her body, face and vaginal area were sore from being assaulted.

She couldn't believe she had been raped and that Samir ordered the rape as a warning to her and her family. She reached in the zip-lock bag that held her things and pulled out Maurice's cell phone that she had taken when he went into surgery. She was happy as hell that it still had battery life. She could feel where her right eye was swelling and she could barely see out of it. She found Jamal's name in the contacts and dialed it. She cleared her throat a couple of times and spat. She could see spots of blood in it. Jamal finally answered after the fourth ring.

"Maurice?" Jamal asked.

"No," Keisha said hoarsely. She cleared her throat.

"Hello?" Jamal spoke into the phone.

Keisha broke down in tears and began crying hysterically.

"Keisha? What's wrong? Is Mar okay?"

"Come get me, Jamal. Please come get me. Please!" Keisha begged in a ragged voice.

"Keisha, what is wrong? Did they release you? Is Maurice okay?"

"They released me. But Samir left me a message," Keisha said hoarsely.

Jamal was silent as his heart pounded in his chest. "Where are you?"

Keisha looked around. Her vision was blurry so she closed her eyes. "I don't know. A church not too far from the police station on Old York Road. I can't really see..." Keisha trailed off and started crying again.

Jamal didn't like the way she sounded. He closed his eyes and took a deep breath. "I'll be there soon, I promise. I'll find you. Just stay put. Tell me what's around you."

"Umm a car dealership and a plaza I think. Just please, hurry." Keisha pleaded. She disconnected the call.

The temperatures had dropped from the lovely warm weather the day started off with. To Keisha, it felt as if the day had gotten colder weather and event wise. She sat on the church steps and started to pray.

11

Jamal looked at his phone after Keisha disconnected the call. He didn't like the way that she sounded and he certainly didn't like the idea that Samir had sent her a message.

"Are Keisha and Maurice okay?" Deisha asked him.

Jamal was silent for a moment. "I don't know," he mumbled. "Take a ride with me. Keisha just asked me to come and get her and I don't like the way that she sounded. I've got a bad feeling."

"Bad feeling like what?" Deisha asked as she grabbed her coat and slipped on her shoes.

"I don't know. But we need to hurry up."

They rushed from Deisha's condo and hurried to Jamal's car. He made his way to Jenkintown as quickly as possible, grateful that the expressway was empty on a Tuesday night. He drove to the police station and then did a search on Google Maps for nearby churches. Rectory Church and Grace Presbyterian were close by. He drove to Rectory first. He saw Keisha sitting on the steps with her head down. She appeared to be shivering. Jamal parked his Impala and got out. He walked over to Keisha and tapped her on her shoulder. She jumped, looking as if she were going to scream. When she recognized Jamal, she threw her arms around him and sobbed loudly. Jamal hugged her back and she collapsed in his arms.

"Keisha, talk to me. What happened?" Jamal asked.

Deisha was watching from the car and noticed Keisha's clothes looked raggedy. She got out of the car and started walking to her when she saw the dry blood on Keisha's thigh.

"Jamal…" Deisha said breathlessly. She pointed to Keisha's leg. Jamal looked down and then pulled Keisha away from him. She tried to look away but he grabbed her face and looked at her. He winced when he saw the bruise on her face and her eye which was nearly swollen shut.

"Who the fuck did this to you, Keisha? What the fuck happened?" Jamal nearly growled. He had a good idea.

"They said if I said anything they would finish Manny off and kill me, too!" Keisha said in a husky voice.

"What did they do to you?" Jamal asked slower. He felt anger taking over him.

Keisha looked at him for a space of heartbeats. "They raped me…" Keisha replied.

Deisha put her hands to her face and bent over in tears. She shook her head as she looked at Keisha and then looked at Jamal. Jamal was furious and she could see it in his face. Deisha had not seen that look in his eyes since Tamera had been murdered.

"Get in the car. I'm taking you to the hospital," Jamal ordered.

"No, I just want to go home," Keisha protested.

"No! You are *going* to the hospital. Don't debate me. Look at your fucking face! I can't believe he did this shit to you. I can't believe Samir went this far," he seethed.

"Samir didn't rape me. One of the cops did at the precinct. He raped me in the cell after he claimed I was being released. I just want to shower. I can… I can still smell his cologne and his sweat and feel where he…" Keisha trailed off and rubbed her hands roughly across the cheek that her attacker licked.

"Jamal, bring her back to my place. She can get showered and cleaned up and I'll bandage her up and everything," Deisha suggested.

Jamal stared at her as he thought it over. "Fine, let's go."

Yani

They got into the car and drove back to Deisha's place as Keisha told Deisha and Jamal everything that happened from the ambush at her apartment to the rape in her holding cell.

Deisha put her arm around Keisha and hugged her close as she wiped the tears from her eyes. She couldn't believe Keisha had endured so much in one day.

"How am I supposed to see my son like this? My mom is going to trip. My mom? Shit, if Manny or Maurice sees me like this…" Keisha trailed off.

"They won't see you like this, don't worry." Jamal assured her.

"But Maurice and Manny are going to want to know why I haven't been up to see them. This black eye won't be gone by tomorrow. Oh my God!" Keisha practically shrieked.

"What, what's wrong?" Jamal asked as he pulled into the garage of Deisha's condo.

"The key, I never got what Manny told me to get from our apartment. What if it's too late?" Keisha replied.

"We'll get it tomorrow. We can't go back tonight." They went up to Deisha's condo and went inside. "Keisha, tell me exactly what the cop said to you."

Deisha fixed an ice pack and gave it to Keisha to put on her eye. Keisha waved it away. "If you don't mind, I really want to take a shower and get this shit off of me."

Deisha reached inside of her hallway closet and pulled out a towel, wash cloth, and an extra bar of soap as well as a bathrobe for Keisha. As she was handing it to her she asked, "Keisha... the cop that... did he use protection?"

Keisha looked at the floor. "No," she said in a soft voice.

Deisha closed her eyes and shook her head. "Keisha, you have to go to the hospital. You need a full STD panel of blood work done as well as an HIV test. You also need to let them do a rape kit in case he ejaculated inside of you, they can pull his records from his DNA and arrest that bastard!"

"Deisha, he's a cop! He raped me in a holding cell and even though I was screaming at the top of my lungs for somebody to come and help me, nobody did! If they can sit by and do nothing while it was happening, what makes you think they'll do something if I report it! Samir threatened to dump my body on my mother's door step if I told!" Keisha said as she trembled. Tears spilled out of her eyes.

Jamal put his hands on her shoulders. "Keisha, even if you don't report it, just let them do the blood work and get a morning after pill. If they start questioning you, they can't make you report anything, okay? But please, get checked out."

Keisha looked at Jamal and then looked at Deisha. They both saw the 15 year old girl who was devastated over Dominique's murder nine years prior. They hugged her and then she made her way to the bathroom to take her shower.

Jamal looked around Deisha's condo while she fixed them both a drink. "This is a really nice place you have here, Deisha."

Deisha passed him a drink. "Thanks. I love it up here; close to my job, great view of the city."

Jamal drank from his glass. "You have a lot of space in here…" he looked at her as if he were studying her. Deisha stared back at him and then looked away. She knew what he was hinting at; a spacious living area yet she lived alone, no boyfriend, no children.

"I'm just getting into my career. There's no room for me to settle down, let alone have children,"

Deisha explained as she plopped down onto the couch.

"I never saw anyone study as much as you in high-school, yet you and Maurice stayed together. He was patient with you. He waited for you because he loved you. He was there all through undergrad and when you got your Master's degree," Jamal replied as he leaned against her fire place.

"That was then. This is now. Things change. I've changed," she replied quietly.

"You were scared. Nothing wrong with that."

Deisha looked up at him. "Psychology is my area of expertise. Please don't psycho-analyze me."

"I wouldn't dream of it. All I'm saying is; life is too short for regrets. You keep running from your past and you'll miss your future. Trust me. I know," Jamal said sadly. He looked over at the picture on Deisha's wall of all of them after graduation. Deisha looked at it too as she thought about what he said.

"I miss her, too," she said softly. She looked at her watch and then grabbed her MacBook. "I promised Chanda I would Skype with her."

"Yeah? I haven't talked to her and Shawn in a while. I haven't seen my niece and nephew in a while, either." Jamal said as he sat on the couch with her.

Deisha saw that Chanda was on Skype and she sent a request for a cam session. Chanda answered with her two year old daughter Amber and four year old son Andre- named after Shawn and Jamal's father. Little

Andre was the splitting image of Shawn and Amber
looked like a mini lighter version of Chanda. They
waved at Deisha not seeing Jamal sitting nearby.

"Hey girl!! It's about time. I've been sitting here
waiting for you. I said; I know this cow did not go to
sleep and she owes me a Skype session." She and
Deisha laughed together.

"No, it's been so much going on over here. It's
been a long day and a rough night," Deisha explained.
"I have someone here who wants to see you." Deisha
turned her MacBook so Jamal was in view. He waved
to Chanda and his niece and nephew.

"Oh my God! JAMAL!!! Wave to your Uncle
Mally, Dre and Amb! Shawn!! Come here!" Chanda
yelled. Deisha and Jamal laughed out loud. Shawn came
into the room in a pair of shorts. He looked bigger than
the last time Deisha saw him; more muscular and she
noticed he had two tattoos on his chest.

Shawn looked at the computer screen. "Oh shit! Is
that Jamal?" Shawn exclaimed.

"Yeah man, it's me. What's good?" Jamal smiled.
Besides the occasional emails, Shawn and Jamal hadn't
seen each other much since Shawn left to play
Basketball in Italy five years prior. They mostly played
phone tag with each other, neither of them adjusting
well to the time difference. They talked and cracked

jokes for a little while before Chanda finally asked what was on her and Shawn's mind.

"What are you doing in Philly, Mal? Shit, somebody must've died to get your ass back in Killadelphia," Chanda laughed. The expressions on Deisha and Jamal's face stopped her laughter. "Oh my God… something happened?" she asked. Jamal looked at Deisha and she looked at him. Jamal figured he better break the bad news. "Kiree was killed. Him and Manny got caught in a shoot-out on 24th and Oxford. Kiree didn't make it and Manny is in the hospital in pretty bad shape. Maurice called me and asked me to come back to Philly because of a favor Keisha needed. When I got to Keisha and Manny's apartment, they were getting ambushed."

"Got-damn! Are they alright!?" Chanda exclaimed with her hand over her chest.

Jamal looked down and shook his head. "Maurice was shot. Keisha killed one of the gunmen and was arrested but they released her."

"Get the fuck outta here!" Chanda shouted. Shawn put his hand over her mouth.

"Yo, what did I tell you about dropping the "f" bomb around the kids? Chill," Shawn told her.

"My bad. Damn is Maurice alright? Where is Keisha?" Chanda asked.

"She's here in the shower. It's a lot going on but I can't get into it right now. Just be glad that y'all ain't here."

Shawn looked at his brother and could tell it was more to the story than just that. For Jamal to be back in Philly, something besides Maurice getting shot was seriously wrong.

"Damn. Give my love to Keisha, Manny and Maurice. I know Ms. Becky gotta be outta her mind right now," Chanda said as she shook her head in sorrow.

Jamal hesitated. "Ms. Becky passed away. After she heard what happened to Kiree and Manny, she had a heart attack and died about an hour afterwards."

Chanda shook her head again. "Damn, it's crazy out there."

"Do they know who did it?" Shawn asked.

Jamal looked at Shawn for a moment and then lowered his eyes. Shawn knew the answer without his brother saying it. He shook his head in anger. Chanda caressed his face and kissed him on the cheek. Deisha noticed a ring on her finger.

"Is that what I think it is?" Deisha asked excitedly.

Chanda looked at the ring and then held her hand up. "YES!! That's what I've been trying to get your ass…" she looked at Shawn quickly and saw the evil eye he was giving her. "…I mean; I was trying to get your butt on Skype so I could give you the good news. Shawn proposed! And I said yes!" Chanda and Deisha squealed.

"Congratulations you two!! I'm so happy for you. Aww! Are you going to come back to Philly to get married or are you going to do it in Italy?" Deisha asked.

"We were talking about coming home to get married sometime next spring," Chanda gushed excitedly.

Shawn noticed a look of worry on Jamal's face. "Babe, take Dre and Amb in the kitchen and fix them some cereal real quick."

Chanda was going to protest but realized it was something he needed to say that he didn't want her or their children to hear. She kissed him and then whisked the children away to the kitchen like she was told.

"Talk to me, Jamal." Shawn said.

"I can't. Not like this. I need you to do me a favor though. Don't come back to Philly for a while." Jamal requested.

Shawn studied him. "Jamal, I promised Mommy I would be home for Thanksgiving and Christmas. She hasn't seen Amber yet."

Jamal cut him off. "I mean it, Shawn. Stay in Italy until I tell you it's cool to come home. I've never been more serious than I am right now. I need you to stay in Italy. Keep you, Chanda and my niece and nephew out of harm's reach. Just do me that one solid," Jamal said sternly.

Shawn hesitated for a moment. "Okay. I got you."

Jamal let out a sigh of relief. "Kiss my niece and nephew for me. Tell Chanda I said congrats. Congrats to you for finally making that move. It's about time, nigga. I'm proud of you."

"Thanks. And I will. Tell Mommy I love her. And keep me updated on Maurice. What hospital is he in?"

"Abington Memorial," Jamal replied.

"Shit, at least it ain't Temple." He and Jamal chuckled. "Alright y'all, I gotta get ready for practice. Stay in touch."

They waved to each other and then disconnected the Skype connection.

"I noticed you didn't tell Shawn about Samir," Deisha said as she closed her MacBook and sat it on the floor.

"I didn't need to. He knows." Jamal stood and stretched. "It's getting late. I'ma head on outta here."

"This time of night? Where are you going to go?" Deisha asked as she took their glasses into the kitchen and placed them inside of her dishwasher.

Jamal thought for a moment. "You know, I didn't think about it until you asked me. I guess I'll grab a room down at one of the hotels near here."

Deisha sucked her teeth. "You don't have to do that. My couch pulls out into a sofa bed. I have some extra blankets and everything. You can stay here."

"You're sure? Where is Keisha going to sleep?"

"I have a spare room with a full size bed. She's probably in there sleeping already." Deisha said as she went down the hall. She peeped in the room and saw Keisha in the bed under the covers. She looked closer to make sure she was asleep. Deisha could tell that she cried herself to sleep. She gently brushed her hair out of her face and kissed her forehead. "You'll be okay. I've got your back and so does Jamal. We won't let anything else happen to you, Manny, Maurice or Kamir." She left back out of the bedroom and made her way back to the living room. Jamal was sitting on her sofa with his head leaned back and his arm over his head. She could tell that he was exhausted.

"Tomorrow morning I'm going to see Maurice and my mom. If she's knows I'm back in Philly but didn't stop by, she'll drive all the way to Delaware and bust my head to the white meat." They chuckled together.

Deisha leaned into the wall and played with her nails. "Jamal… did you mean what you said earlier when you said that Maurice still loves me?" she asked innocently.

Jamal looked at her. "Yes. He loves you and misses you. And y'all both need to stop acting so damn hard and just kiss and make-up."

Deisha shook her head. "I'm not sure it will be that easy. What I did was…"

"I know about the abortion. And I know he asked you to marry him and you turned him down. Don't get me wrong, that hurt my man. Like that shit really did hurt his heart. He wanted y'all to be a family.

"See Deisha, what you never understood was; Maurice will never let you take on anything alone. He'll always be there for you no matter what. You should've known that when Raheem was killed and he stayed with you every day to make sure you were okay."

Deisha was close to tears. "I'm just so afraid to end up like my mom. I'm so scared that no matter how strong I am, no matter how successful I become, having a baby will show just how weak I am, like her. And I don't want that." She sniffed and wiped her face.

"You're not her, Deisha. And Maurice will never leave you to raise his child by yourself. You just need to learn to trust him and believe in him. Don't let him getting shot make you realize that losing him was a mistake. Fix it before it's too late. And don't keep saying tomorrow. Because tomorrow isn't always promised." Jamal was kicking knowledge to Deisha.

Deisha nodded her head in agreement. She then smiled. "Now look at whose giving advice. Who died and made you Negrodamous?" They laughed together. "What if he's seeing someone else?" she asked.

"He's not. Trust me." Jamal smiled at her vulnerability.

Deisha nodded again and then took a deep breath. "Thank God I don't have any early morning sessions or appointments tomorrow. I'm gonna shower and head to bed. Blankets, sheets, towels and wash cloths are all in the closet. If you're hungry, there's some left over Spaghetti in the refrigerator. Thanks so much, Jamal. It's really good to see you."

"You're welcome. It's good to see you, too," Jamal replied. Deisha turned to go take her shower and Jamal looked around again. He walked over to the large photo of them from graduation and stared at Tamera. He stared at the photo for a long time and thought back to their last moments together as he began to play with her ring that hung around his neck. The images of that day were still fresh and vivid in his memory as if they had happened just days before. He then remembered rushing into Hahnemann Hospital and seeing Shawn with the bloody white t-shirt on. He shook his head to clear that image from his mind's eye and let out a deep sigh. He held the ring between his fingers and kissed it. "I miss you, Tammy… so much."

12

The loud ringing of Deisha's house phone snatched Jamal from his sleep. He rolled from the sofa bed and moved toward the cordless phone so he could take it to her.

"Yes," Deisha groaned as she sat up in her bed.

"The phone homie, are you decent?" Jamal asked.

"Yeah, I'm good. Bring it to me, please."

Jamal covered his eyes and walked into the room. Deisha laughed as she took the phone from him. She answered just as the answering machine picked up.

"Hello, hello?" she said loudly to make sure the person on the other end knew she had answered and didn't hang up.

"Yes Ms. Burton, this is Mr. Boykin from the lobby. There's a woman here by the name of Charlene Brown demanding I let her up to your residence."

"Charlene Brown?" Deisha asked in confusion. That was Maurice and Keisha's mother. *How the hell did she find me?* Deisha thought to herself. "I know her, Grant. But I'm not decent. Shit," Deisha sprung from her bed and threw on her robe. She signaled for Jamal to come back to her and put her hand over the mouth piece to her phone.

"What's wrong?" Jamal asked.

"Maurice and Keisha's mom is downstairs trying to get my doorman to let her up here! What are we going to tell her about Keisha?" Deisha asked hastily.

"Ms. Burton?" Deisha heard Mr. Boykin on her phone.

"Yes Grant, I'm still here. Um send her up in about ten minutes. I just want to brush my teeth and throw some clothes on."

Mr. Boykin turned his back to a very angry and concerned Ms. Brown. "Ms. Burton uh… she's a tad upset I'm not sure if she's going to go for that."

"I know Ms. Brown can be a pit-bull, trust me, I've had run-ins with her too many times. As a matter of fact, put her on the phone." Deisha quickly put on a pair of sweat pants and an Immaculata University t-shirt.

"Deisha?" a woman's voice said on the phone.

"Yes, Ms. Brown. Good morning. How can I help you?" She signaled to Jamal to fold up her sofa bed and get dressed.

"How am I? How am I?! My son has been shot! My daughter's thug boyfriend has also been shot! I'm hearing she killed someone and was arrested but when

I called the police station, I was told that she had been released, yet I have not heard from her. I went to her apartment. There's yellow caution tape across the door to her apartment and she isn't there! I can't find my grandson! I'm going out of my damn mind. How do you think I am?" Ms. Brown snapped. She sounded as if she were close to tears.

"Ms. Brown I understand…" Deisha started to respond but was interrupted.

"Listen Deisha, I didn't drive down here to speak with you over the phone. I need to come up and see you in person."

Deisha closed her eyes and took a deep breath. "Yes, of course. Just sign the visitor's log, show Grant your ID and he'll let you right up. I'm on the 12th floor. My condo is 1216."

Ms. Brown handed the phone back to Mr. Boykin.

"You were right, she is a pit-bull," he whispered into the handset as Ms. Brown dug for her driver's license.

"I told you," Deisha said in a sing-song manner as she put tooth-paste onto her tooth-brush. They giggled together and then hung up. Deisha quickly brushed her teeth and splashed water onto her face.

"You want me to leave now? I'm not sure how Maurice's mom will feel seeing her son's best friend in her son's ex-girlfriend's condo," Jamal said as he stood in the bathroom doorway.

"Her misconception is the last thing on my mind right now. I'm more concerned with how the fuck am I going to explain Keisha's black eye," Deisha replied as she pat-dry her face with a wash cloth. She tidied up the bathroom and did a quick surveillance of her living room and kitchen before Ms. Brown arrived. Just as she was wiping down her sink and straightening her dish towels on their racks, her door-bell rang.

"You look nervous," Jamal said with a smirk on his face.

"I haven't seen his mom in almost four years. I'm wondering if she knows…" Deisha trailed off.

"No. Maurice never told her."

Deisha did a cross over her chest. "Thank God." Her doorbell rang again and she went over to her door and opened it. She was shocked when Ms. Brown grabbed her and hugged her. She hugged her back hesitantly and then showed her inside.

"Deisha, I know we've had our differences in the past and I wasn't exactly the kindest person in the world to you, but I am at the end of my rope. I need answers. I need help." Ms. Brown said as she tried her best to maintain her usual voice and not shed a tear. She then noticed Jamal. "Oh my God! Jamal! I had no idea you were here. You must have heard about Maurice."

Deisha and Jamal looked at each other not sure what to tell her and what to keep quiet. Jamal decided to take the lead.

"Ms. Brown, what do you know and what are you trying to find out?" he asked.

Deisha offered a seat to Ms. Brown on the love seat. "Would you like a cup of coffee or tea?"

Ms. Brown waved her hand, declining. Deisha sat next to Jamal on the sofa.

Ms. Brown let out a shaky sigh. "All I know is Manny was shot and his brother was killed. I was trying to reach Keisha on her cell-phone to see if she was okay but I kept getting her voice-mail. Then someone came banging on my door last night saying Keisha had been arrested for killing someone and Maurice had been shot! I still haven't seen him because no one knows what hospital he's in!" She put her hands to her face trying to keep calm.

Jamal took a deep breath. "Yes, Kiree was killed and Manny was injured as well. Maurice reached out to me and asked me to come to Philly because Keisha needed a favor."

"A favor for what?" Ms. Brown interrupted him.

"Ms. Brown, let me finish," Jamal said. Ms. Brown apologized and took a deep breath, trying to calm herself down. Too much had gone on in the last 24 hours and she had hardly gotten any sleep the night before. She was eager to find her son and daughter as well as her grandson to make sure they were all okay.

Jamal took a deep breath as well and continued. "When I got to Philly, I called Maurice back and Keisha asked that I meet them at her apartment in Jenkintown. When I got there, they were getting ambushed."

"Oh dear God!" Ms. Brown said as she put a trembling hand to her mouth.

"I heard the gun-shots and immediately drew my weapon. I put down one of the attackers. The other attacker had already been taken down by Keisha and Maurice had already been shot." Jamal explained. He fell silent and looked at the floor. "If only I had gotten there sooner…"

"My baby killed someone," Ms. Brown sobbed. "Where is Maurice?"

"He's at Abington Memorial Hospital. And Ms. Brown, it was self-defense. Keisha did what she had to do. They were attacked in her home. If she had not done what she did, both of your children could be dead," Deisha said.

Ms. Brown cried for a moment and Deisha handed her a tissue. "Where is Keisha now?"

Deisha and Jamal were silent for a moment. Deisha shook her head and said, "She's here sleeping. She called after she was released late last night and asked if Jamal would come pick her up."

"Oh thank God, she's okay. I don't understand why she didn't call me. I would have come to get her." She noticed the looks on Jamal and Deisha's faces. "What aren't you telling me?"

"I can bring her home if you want, Ms. Brown. I don't have any clients today so it wouldn't be a problem at all," Deisha said quickly.

"No, I want her to leave now so we can go get her son and then see Maurice. He shouldn't be at that hospital alone with no family or friends," Ms. Brown replied.

"Ms. Brown, please if you could just wait a little longer," Jamal started.

"No! If she is in here sleeping, you tell her to come out here right now!" Ms. Brown said angrily. She didn't understand why Jamal and Deisha were stalling.

"Can you wait right here? I'll go wake her." Deisha went down the hallway and disappeared inside of her guest bedroom. Keisha was already awake sitting in the bed with her back against the head board. The bruise on her eye had magnified and the swelling had barely gone down. It was no way they would be able to explain that to Ms. Brown without her having a shit attack.

"I'm not going out there," Keisha said as she shook her head.

"Oh Keisha," Deisha said as she sat next to her on the bed. She looked at her young friend sorrowfully and shook her head. "Your mom is so worried about you and Maurice and your son. I know Samir threatened you but the only way to stop him is to tell what happened. Jamal can protect you. We all can protect you."

"Yeah, like he protected Tammy?" Keisha said as she looked at Deisha with tears in her eyes. "I can't say anything. I have no proof. It will be my word against that cop's and it won't even get to Samir because I have no proof that he threatened me or made that fucking cop rape me. Y'all can't help me."

Deisha tried to move her hair out of her face but Keisha flinched and moved away. "Keisha, you know how your mom is. I can't keep her from seeing you.

She will bust down this door and I don't too much blame her considering everything that happened yesterday."

"What am I supposed to tell her?" Keisha asked in a shaky voice.

"The truth," Deisha suggested.

"I CAN'T!" Keisha yelled. She shook her head and tried swallowing past the knot of sadness, anger and fear in her throat. "My son lost his uncle. He damn near lost his father. He's not going to lose me and I won't jeopardize his life either."

They sat quiet for a moment. Deisha didn't know what to say for she had never faced anything significantly close to what Keisha had endured in the last 24 hours. Sorry didn't cut it and no form of apology could right any of the wrongs that transpired. Instead, she grabbed Keisha by her hand and held it.

"Keesh, as a mother you know if your son was in trouble, nothing and no one would keep you from him. You know how your mother is and I am positive that in two minutes, she is going to break down this door if you don't come out of this room so that she can physically see you are okay. She is worried sick! Of all people to reach out to, she came to me. Me! You may not want to tell your mother the truth about what was done to you right now but no matter what you tell her, I will be there with you every step of the way. And so will Jamal," Deisha said as she squeezed Keisha's hand.

Keisha waited a moment before nodding her head in agreement. She climbed from the bed and she and Deisha walked from the room hand in hand. Keisha looked at the floor not wanting to see the look of horror on her mother's face once her bruises were seen.

Ms. Brown stood up feeling relieved until she saw the bruises on Keisha's face and her swollen eye. "Keisha! What the hell happened to your face? Who did this to you?!" she asked hysterically as she hurried over to her. She grabbed her face so she could get a closer look.

"I'm alright, mom. I'm fine," Keisha replied trying to turn away.

"You're not fine. Is this why you were stalling, Deisha? Somebody better tell me what the hell is going on and right now!" Ms. Brown demanded.

Deisha was silent. Jamal looked at Deisha and then looked at Keisha. He was getting ready to speak but Keisha stopped him.

"It's just silly, petty, street drama, mom. Some neighborhood chick found out about Manny and Kiree and came up to the hospital claiming to have been messing with Manny for the last six months. We got into a little scuffle and well…" Keisha trailed off and looked at Jamal and Deisha. "My face doesn't look nearly as bad as hers and that's only because she snuck me. But I'm fine," she gave her mother a nervous smile and quickly looked away.

Ms. Brown looked at her daughter suspiciously not believing one word she was saying. She could see the guilty expressions on all of their faces but she left that topic alone for the moment. Her primary concern was the fact that an attempt was made on her daughter's life as well as her son's. Not to mention, her daughter had taken someone else's life.

"I told you that boy was bad news. Now look at what's happened; his brother is dead, he's laid up in the hospital, your brother's been shot and you... oh baby. You killed a man!" Ms. Brown tried to hug Keisha but she crabbed up and moved away.

"And I would do it again in a heartbeat. Anybody that threatens my life, my son's or my brother's will get the same," Keisha said coldly. Her mother had never seen that kind of gleam in her eye before.

Ms. Brown cleared her throat. "Well, you need to contact your job and talk to your boss to make sure you don't lose your position. And then get cleaned up so we can go get Kamir and see Maurice."

"I already spoke to my boss. They are giving me an FMLA for six weeks. They are going to mail the paper work to me, I just have to fill it out and send it back. Kamir is with Angie." Keisha explained.

"He should be with you," Ms. Brown stated.

"Mom, I know you mean well but there is just so much going on in my mind right now. I need a moment to get myself together. I'll meet you up at Abington to see Maurice around 1 o'clock."

"Keisha…" Ms. Brown tried to argue.

"Mom, please." Keisha said as she continued to avoid eye contact.

Ms. Brown was disappointed in her daughter's behavior. She knew something was going on and did not appreciate being kept in the dark about whatever it was. She hugged her daughter tightly and then kissed her on the cheek. She looked at the bruise on her face again and shook her head in disgust. "I love you, baby. 1 o'clock. And not a minute later, okay?"

"Of course mom," Keisha managed a smile.

Deisha walked Ms. Brown to the door. "It was good seeing you, Ms. Brown."

"It was good seeing you too, Deisha. You have a beautiful home. I'm glad you turned out to be an accomplished young lady. I hope to see you at Abington Hospital later today."

"Absolutely," Deisha smiled. She was shocked that Ms. Brown had been so kind to her. She closed and locked the door behind her.

"That could've been a lot worse," Jamal said as he looked at Keisha. "Are you okay?"

"Not by a long shot," Keisha said as she looked up at him. "I need one of you to take me back to my apartment. I need to get Manny's money and the keys to the house in Glenolden."

"After you get checked out at the hospital. And don't debate me, Keisha. I didn't say anything when you told that bold-faced lie to your mom. But you are going to the hospital to get checked out. Jefferson isn't too far from here. I already have a change of clothes for you," Deisha said as she made her way back to her bedroom. Keisha sighed not really wanting to go through the ordeal but she figured she had worse things to face. There was no way she could go without seeing Manny and Maurice today and they both would want to know what happened to her. There also was no way she could tell them the same lie she told her mother. They wouldn't believe it.

13

Detective Davidson spent most of the night looking through Jamal's file. He wasn't finding what he was looking for and it was beginning to frustrate him. He knew it was there somewhere in the contents of that folder, he just needed to see it. It wasn't until almost six in the morning that he had fallen asleep in his recliner with the file on his lap. He shifted in his sleep causing the file to fall on the floor and woke up. He picked the folder and its contents up when something caught his attention. He was so busy trying to find answers in Jamal's file that he never thought to look in Shawn's file. He then had an idea. What if what he was looking for wasn't in Jamal's file but in Shawn's? He put on a pot of coffee and called the female officer that retrieved Jamal's information for him.

"Hey Jessica, this is Keith. I need you to check on something for me. Can you see if there is anything on a Shawn Williams? He's the younger brother of Jamal Williams," he asked once the officer answered.

"Luckily for you I just sat down at my desk. Are you coming in?" Jessica asked as she opened a few of her systems and waited for them to load up.

"Yeah, but I need to do some field work first. We actually should have something on Shawn. Jamal was shot back in 2000 and there was a situation with a gun but Shawn was never charged."

"Give me one second. What's his date of birth? We have a lot of Shawn Williams in here."

Davidson grabbed the folder from the counter and flipped through it. "October 24th 1984," he told her before tossing the folder onto the counter. He grabbed his coffee mug from his cabinet and fixed his coffee just the way he liked it; black, no cream and just three sugars to balance out its strength. The smell of his Almond flavored Maxwell House awakened him and made him feel refreshed and rejuvenated despite his lack of sleep. He took a deep whiff of it as if the hot caffeinated beverage were a drug, and then blew softly into the mug before taking a sip as he waited patiently for Jessica to pull up what he needed.

"Okay, looks like you were right," Jessica said. "Shawn Williams was 16 years old when he was brought in for questioning for the December 9th shooting of his brother Jamal Williams. He was also questioned about a gun that apparently had his finger prints on it. The said gun was not the one used in Jamal's shooting so he was cleared of that. He was never charged for possession of a weapon either. Shawn stated that the gun was found in a lot on his way home and he didn't know what to do with it so he kept it." Jessica scanned through the write-up. "Hmm, that's interesting."

"What?" Davidson asked.

"Apparently, Shawn was released but the gun they linked back to him, a .45 caliber hi-power Derringer, was traced back to Khalil Dixon's murder. Shawn was never brought up on charges because when IAB was doing their transport, they were raided which resulted in two Federal Officers being killed and all merchandise was seized. With no weapon, all pending charges against Shawn were dropped September 8th 2002."

Davidson became quiet. He remembered that raid. More than 40 weapons had been confiscated along with cocaine, heroin and marijuana. The heat came down on the security detail of that transport as well as IAB. The assumption was that the leak came straight from IAB and not the department. He leaned on the counter with his hands to his face. This shit was deeper than he anticipated.

"Who was in charge of that transport?" Davidson asked after a moment of silence.

"Umm let's see," Jessica said. Davidson could hear her typing. "Sergeant Alekzander Kristoff of IAB;

He was killed in 2010 after leaving his home. His throat was slit. It wasn't ruled as a robbery because his credit cards, cash and his wedding ring had not been stolen. Case is still under investigation," Jessica replied.

"Got damn it," Davidson mumbled. "Fax that file to me ASAP." He gave her his fax number and hung up.

Davidson picked up the sheet from Jamal's file that had grabbed his attention and prompted him to adjust his manner of research. He drank down his coffee that had cooled a bit as he stared at the paper.

"What's done in the dark…" he said to himself. He heard the fax machine go off and went over to it. He collected each paper as it came through and fixed himself another cup of coffee before going to his desk. He spread the papers out and grabbed his tablet to write down notes as he read. After an hour, he looked over his notes and turned on his tape recorder.

"This all goes back to Raheem Powell's murder in July 1998. Raheem was friends with Jamal and Shawn. Khalil allegedly killed Raheem for whatever reason; accident- maybe the bullet was meant for Jamal but Raheem was caught instead. Let's say that Jamal feels guilty and kills Khalil. At 15 years old, he needed help. Maybe that's where Samir comes in. Now we go to December 2000; Shawn finds the gun and takes it.

Jamal gets into an altercation and is shot. Shawn drops the gun which is how it lands in police custody. A .45 caliber hi-power Derringer is only issued to cops. Shawn got the gun from Jamal, Jamal got the gun from Samir, and Samir got the gun from a cop. But which cop; Johnson, Parker or Kristoff? Shawn is never charged for possession of a weapon because of the IAB transport raid; a transport that was led by Kristoff. Khalil and Raheem's murders are left unsolved, both cases closed. Johnson and Parker never arrested Jamal, but processed his paper work and signed off on his release. Both were killed. But how does Kristoff factor in?" Davidson stopped the tape recorder and sat thinking. He was positive Khalil Dixon killed Raheem Powell which was the reason Jamal killed him. He was also positive that Samir helped Jamal carry out the hit and Samir was getting major pull from the Philadelphia Police; from rookies all the way up to IAB. No wonder he had been untouchable for so long. The only problem was with Kristoff, Johnson and Parker dead, who the hell was helping Samir now? He began gathering the papers together so he could put them back in the folder when his phone rang. He saw that Jamal was calling him.

"This is Detective Davidson," he answered.

"I need to see you," Jamal said.

"See me for what, Jamal? I thought you were on the first thing out of here?" Davidson smirked with sarcasm.

"You can either agree to meet with me, or I will be on the first thing out of here. It won't take much for me to change my mind," Jamal retorted.

"Do you know where Regency House Apartments are?" Davidson asked. "Yeah, over on 10th Street not too far from Fern Rock Train Station."

"How soon can you get here?" Davidson asked.

"Give me an hour. I'm on my way to visit my mom." Jamal disconnected the call.

Davidson closed his eyes. He believed he was onto something and hoped whatever it was allowed him to take down Samir as well as any dirty cop that was involved with him.

14

As Jamal drove through his old neighborhood, the memories of his teenage years flooded his mind; old friends that he hung out with, playing basketball with his younger brother Shawn, long walks that he would take with Tamera hand in hand. He came from one of the worst areas in the city and got caught up in some of the worst possible situations that would normally break a person with less strength, mentally. He counted his blessings that he didn't fall prey to the stereo-typical endings that most of his other friends had fallen prey to; death, prison sentences, life time hustlers too ignorant to find a better life for themselves. He only wished that Tamera and his daughter had made it out unharmed. That one critical failure would haunt him for the rest of his life.

He parked outside of his mother's home. She had made quite a few changes using the money that both he and Shawn sent to her on a regular basis. The front walls of the house were now adorned with cream colored aluminum siding with chocolate brown trimming. A matching chocolate brown awning with cream trimming the same color as the aluminum siding peeked out over the front porch which had now been fully cemented and decorated with multiple flower pots. Even though his mother's house was in the heart of the ghetto plagued with violence, drugs and despair; seeing the front of her house gave Jamal a sense of hope that the neighborhood could change and its current state did not have to be a permanent state. He looked around and noticed that a few of the neighbors tried following her lead. Though they didn't have the fancy décor on their homes, they had potted plants to make the block more cheerful. Jamal also noticed there was no trash on the ground; not even so much as a leaf blew in the wind.

It took him a moment to walk onto his mother's porch. He reached inside of his jacket pocket wondering if his key still worked. He knew she was home, having memorized her schedule in case a day like this came. He timidly opened the glass storm door and stuck his key in the top lock. He was shocked that it turned. He twisted the door knob and it opened. He then wished that he had brought her some flowers, or a Pepsi, or something. Showing up at her home empty handed after being gone for more than nine years seemed disrespectful.

He looked around and then looked at the stairs almost jumping out of his skin when he saw his mother pointing a .22 caliber pistol at him. He jumped back and threw his hands up.

"Mom it's me! Don't shoot!" he said as he breathed heavily.

"Jamal! Oh my God!" his mother exclaimed. She put the safety on her gun, sat it on the dining room table and hugged her son tightly. They held each other for a moment before finally letting one another go.

"Mom, what are you doing with a gun?" Jamal asked as he picked it up and checked to make sure it was loaded correctly.

Ms. Keyona looked at him sideways. "Boy, do you NOT see where I live?" They laughed together. "I heard about Maurice. I'm so sorry. Is that why you're in Philly?"

"No, actually I got here before he was shot. It's a long story. There's so much going on right now, it would be better if you didn't know too much," Jamal explained.

"Police business?" Ms. Keyona asked.

Jamal looked away without responding. "The house looks way different than it did when me and Shawn lived here."

Ms. Keyona smiled at his evasiveness. "Yeah, I had to make a few changes. It took me a while to get used to you and Shawn not being here. But I'm okay now. I was just about to put on a pot of grits and make some bacon and scrambled eggs. You want something to eat?"

"Oh no mom, I'm fine. I just wanted to come see you. I didn't want to be in Philly and not stop by."

"Yeah because I would've came all the way to Delaware and bust your head to the white meat," his mother replied in her best Bernie Mac voice. Jamal laughed out loud. "Come sit down with me and eat. Lord only knows when the next time I'll get the chance to have breakfast in my kitchen with my oldest son."

Jamal was a tad hungry. He had barely eaten anything since before he arrived in Philly. He followed his mother into the kitchen and sat at her table. He looked around at all of the photos she had up of him and Shawn. She even had photos of Shawn and Chanda from Italy as well as a photo of Shawn's son

Andre. It dawned on Jamal that in all of the years he lived in that house, he couldn't think of one time where they all had sat down together and enjoyed a meal. His mother was always at work or he was always running the streets.

Yani

The smell of his mother's home cooked food made his hunger come alive. They talked while they ate with Jamal updating her on how life was treating him in Delaware.

"So how long will you be in Philly?" Ms. Keyona asked as she cleared the table.

Jamal thought about the request that Davidson made and let out a deep sigh. "Longer than I anticipated."

Ms. Keyona studied her son for a moment. She could tell that something was troubling him. She sat down and held his hand. "Whatever brought you back to Philly, I'm grateful because it allowed me a chance to see you. But if you think your visit here will do you more harm than good, don't stay."

"I'm tired of running, mom." Jamal said in a soft voice. He looked at her and Ms. Keyona could see the pain and sorrow in his face.

"You sound like you have some unfinished business," she replied.

Jamal didn't say anything at first. He squeezed her hand and smiled. "I never imagined you having a gun."

"Me neither," Ms. Keyona giggled. "And I pray I never have to use it."

Jamal stood up and thought for a moment. "I pray you don't either, mom. But if you do, shoot to kill, not to injure. Because the other person may not have given you the same courtesy." He glanced at his mother and then looked away. "I have to go meet someone. It was good seeing you, mom."

"It was good seeing you too, honey. Come back and see me sometime. Shawn will be here for Thanksgiving with Chanda and the kids. I was on Skype with them a few days ago and Shawn told me they are engaged. I'm so happy for him and those babies are just gorgeous. If you're still around, you should come also. I bought myself a little digital camera; it would be nice to get some pictures of you all together."

Jamal didn't want to tell his mother that he had already warned Shawn not to come to Philly. He didn't want to disappoint or alarm her. Instead he said, "If I'm not on duty, yeah I'll be here." He gave his mother a hug and squeezed her tightly. "I love you, mom."

"I love you too, baby."

Jamal left out and his mother locked the door behind him. He stepped off the porch and began walking towards his car but stopped dead in his tracks after seeing a man sitting on his hood. The man stared at him and Jamal stared back. It had been more than nine years since Jamal laid eyes on him. Without the dread lox, he looked different. But the eyes were still the same; sharp, intimidating and alert. He smiled at Jamal but Jamal did not smile back.

"It's been a long time, Cousin."

"Not long enough," Jamal said acidly.

Smirking, the individual said, "Don't be like that."

"What do you want, Samir?" Jamal asked. He casually slid his hand behind his back where his gun was.

Samir chuckled loudly. "Think twice, 'Mal." He shifted his vision to the left and Jamal looked in the same direction, seeing a dark skinned individual with a heavy leather jacket on with his hand inside. Samir then shifted his vision to the right and Jamal looked in that direction as well seeing a brown skinned male in an Abercrombie hoody. He lifted it slightly so Jamal could see the chrome 9MM pistol in his pants. Samir then nodded at Jamal. Jamal turned around and saw another dark skinned individual coming towards him with a glock 9 in his hand. Samir laughed out loud and clapped his hands together as his cronie disarmed Jamal and nudged him in Samir's direction.

"Let's take a ride, Jamal. We've got a lot of catching up to do. This ain't a fucking request either.

So move like your muthafucking life depends on it."
Samir said in a threatening tone.

Jamal looked around and weighed his options. He was out numbered with no back up. His only option was to take the ride…and pray.

15

Keisha walked over to Thomas Jefferson Hospital with Deisha. She was nervous as to what she was going to say to the doctors that were going to examine her. At first she contemplated telling the doctors that she wanted the test simply because the condom broke and she just wanted to be safe. But she knew they may possibly question her about the black eye she was sporting. She decided to just say she was assaulted but did not want to report it for personal reasons. She wore her sunglasses inside of the hospital and Deisha walked her over to the nurse's station.

"Hi, I'm here with a friend of mine. She was assaulted last night and wanted to be examined but she doesn't want to file a police report," Deisha said quietly.

The nurse looked at Deisha and then looked at Keisha in her sunglasses. "By assaulted, do you mean raped?" the nurse asked.

"Yes," Deisha replied.

"We have to report all sex crimes to the proper authorities," the nurse said.

"Fuck this, I'm outta here," Keisha mumbled as she turned to walk away. Deisha grabbed her by her arm and pulled her back.

"What if she doesn't want to consent to a rape kit, she just simply wants blood work done to be sure she didn't contract any STDs or HIV?"

The nurse looked at both of them and thought for a moment. She then rose from her seat and signaled for them to follow her. Deisha continued to hold Keisha's hand as they followed behind the nurse. They went inside of a patient room.

"I could get into a lot of trouble for this, but I understand your concern; going through the motions of being poked, prodded, questioned and made to give a detailed account of what happened. If it goes to trial, will the person be convicted? If they aren't convicted, will they attack again? Will you be safe? Then it's the mental and emotional scarring, possible development of intimacy issues and whether or not you will look at all men differently. It's a lot," the nurse said as she pulled out some supplies. She motioned for Keisha to sit down and prepared to take her blood.

"Thank you so much. This really means a lot," Deisha said gratefully.

"Can I ask you a question?" the nurse asked Keisha as she prepped her arm. Keisha nodded. "Did you know your attacker?"

"If I told you or anyone else who did this to me, you wouldn't believe me," Keisha replied, flatly.

"You might be surprised. I've heard all kinds of stories while working at this hospital."

Keisha took a deep breath. "A cop raped me in my holding cell. My brother and I were ambushed at my apartment. They were ordered to kill us after my boyfriend had been shot and his brother was killed. My brother was shot after I shot and killed one of the gunmen. Then I was arrested and held for more than two hours and denied a phone call. A cop came in claiming I was being released. He beat, choked and raped me before warning me that if I told anyone, my body would be dumped on my mother's doorstep," she said.

The nurse didn't respond. She completed the blood work and then placed a band aid on Keisha's arm. "This will be sent to a lab. I just need you to fill out this paper work with your insurance information. If anything abnormal comes back, you'll be contacted. Remember, no news is good news."

Keisha took the paperwork and filled it out as quickly as possible. When she was done and handed it back to the nurse, she looked at her from behind her sunglasses. "You never said whether or not you believed me."

The nurse dumped everything in the trash and collected the tubes of blood. "Yes, I do," she said quietly.

Keisha tilted her sunglasses up enough to wipe the tears from her eyes. "Thank you. Thank you so much."

Deisha and Keisha left the hospital. "See," Deisha said to Keisha as she rubbed her back. "That wasn't as hard as you thought it was going to be."

"No, but things are about to get real ugly. Who are we going to see first; Manny or Maurice?"

"Considering I have some demons of my own to face let's deal with Manny first and then your brother."

They sat in the car outside of Temple University Hospital trying to clean up Keisha's face by applying make-up. Though the bruise's coloring was blending in with the help of the foundation, the swelling around Keisha's eye and the high end of her cheek bone was very visible.

"This is hopeless," Keisha said as she looked at herself in Deisha's vanity mirror while dabbing on a little more foundation. Deisha took out her comb and tried styling Keisha's hair so that some of it fell over her right eye but it was beginning to look obvious that they were trying to hide something.

"I don't know if it looks obvious because I know what happened or if I think it looks obvious just because," Deisha said as she tried to give Keisha a swoop bang. She leaned back so she could take a look at her. Unsatisfied, she sighed and shook her head. "That's the best I can do. You might just have to tell him, Keisha."

"I can't, Deisha. He's recovering from three gunshot wounds not to mention his brother is dead and he still doesn't know his mom passed away. I can't add to the stress," Keisha replied as she angrily tossed her make-up back inside of her hand bag.

Deisha didn't have a response. Instead, she thought that maybe she shouldn't try finding an out for Keisha, but allow her to find her own out and make whatever decisions she felt was best for her and her family.

"Well," Deisha said as she grabbed her purse. "We can't stay in this car forever. Let's go see how Manny is doing."

Just in case, and because Keisha could not bear the stares of on-lookers and the possibility that they could see what she was hiding behind her makeup, she slipped her sunglasses on. They walked into the hospital and over to the receptionist desk to receive visitors' passes to go to Manny's room. When they got up there, Keisha was relieved to see that he was sleeping. So much had happened between the time Manny instructed her to retrieve the money and keys to their other home and this moment. She pulled up a chair beside him and watched him sleep. Moments later, a nurse came in to check his vitals.

"How is he?" Keisha asked.

"So far, he hasn't contracted a fever which is excellent. That's one less battle his body has to fight. His blood pressure was up earlier because he was in a great deal of pain this morning, so we sedated him and put him on a morphine drip. All and all, he's coming along quite nicely," the nurse reassured Keisha with a friendly smile. Keisha thanked her and then held Manny's hand. As vulnerable as she was at that moment, she was doing her best to stay strong for him. She hadn't had a chance to mourn Kiree or their mother. She hadn't even had a chance to come to terms with the fact that her brother was lying in a similar hospital bed across the city also suffering from a gunshot wound and that she had killed a man to save her family. The healing process for the brutal rape that she suffered had not even begun. As far as Keisha was concerned, it wasn't about her at this time. She needed to keep it together for her family and then she would take care of herself.

Keisha leaned her head down and began to pray. Praying seemed to be the only thing that kept her from having a nervous breakdown in the last 24 hours. She felt Manny squeezing her hand so she looked at him. She smiled and Manny smiled back. He searched her face and then slowly reached for the sunglasses. Keisha moved away from his reach to avoid having him take them off. He looked at her strangely as she touched them tentatively.

Manny cleared his throat and licked his lips. "Take off the glasses, I want to see your eyes," he struggled to say.

"I have them on to block out the light. I didn't get much sleep last night and I have a slight migraine," Keisha stammered. She smiled nervously. "I just took something for it though. I'll be okay."

Manny didn't believe her. In his gut, he could tell something was wrong. For the moment, he decided to let it go. He looked around and noticed his mother wasn't there. When he saw Deisha, he gave her a slight thumb's up. Deisha smiled and winked at him in return.

Manny looked back at Keisha and said in a slow manner, "Where's my mom?"

Keisha was prepared for that question. She cleared her throat and said, "You just missed her. She was here while you were sleeping but needed to get home with Kamir and take care of some other things. She told me to tell you that she loves you and will be back to see you later." Keisha lied and felt horrible about it. She was glad that she was wearing the sunglasses so Manny couldn't tell that she was lying. He searched her face but didn't say anything. Instead, he looked up towards the ceiling and closed his eyes.

Keisha shook her head and stood up to leave once Manny fell back to sleep. Deisha followed her out of his room.

"Are you okay?" Deisha asked her as they made their way down the hallway.

"I hate lying to him," Keisha said in tears. She stopped and broke down crying. Deisha put her arms around Keisha and held her as she cried. "This shit is so wrong! So fucking wrong! He's not supposed to be here like this! Kiree and his mom should still be here! Look what they did to me and my fucking brother!" Keisha was near hysterics as she cried.

Deisha shushed her. "Calm down, Keesh. Come on, let's take a walk so you can get some air," she suggested.

"I don't wanna calm down and I don't need to take a walk!" Keisha cried angrily as Deisha continued to hold her. It took a moment for Keisha to collect herself. Deisha passed her some tissues to wipe her face.

When she finished, Keisha said, "Well, that was round one. Are you ready for round two?" she asked Deisha.

Deisha took a deep breath. "Let's do it."

16

Jamal was taken to a warehouse in the uptown section of Philadelphia by Samir and his crew of cronies. He wasn't sure if Samir intended to kill him, scare him, or both. Jamal didn't scare easily after everything he had seen and been through. He was skeptical and optimistic at the same time. He didn't think Samir was going to kill him because it was rare that he did his own dirty work. But he wasn't sure either. He also wasn't sure why he would feel the need to scare him because he had not done anything.

Once inside, Samir leaned onto the edge of a metal table and stared at Jamal for a long time. Jamal stared back.

"Damn, my baby cousin done found his way back to my city," Samir said with a smile on his face. "I thought when you rolled out in '02 that would've been the last I saw or heard from you." Jamal continued to stare at Samir without saying anything. Though he was staring at Samir, he still made a point to know where his goons were in case it came down to him fighting his way out of there. "What are you doing here, 'Mal?"

"Minding my business," Jamal said in a calm tone.

Yani

Samir chuckled along with another one of his guys. "Minding your business," he mocked. "I see you still have a smart-ass mouth."

"And I see you're still making empty threats," Jamal said back quickly.

Samir stared at him for a moment. "I don't make threats; I make promises. Talk to Keisha, lately?" Samir said with a smirk.

Jamal felt a heated fury rising within him. "What kind of bitch-ass comes after a woman? The same bitch-ass who's never man enough to make shit happen on his own; always hiding behind somebody else while they do your dirty work." Jamal shook his head as he looked his cousin up and down.

Samir pointed his gun at him. "You never did know how to show respect. And now look at you; your bitch-ass came all the way back to Philly just to get murked like your pussy ass pop."

Jamal stepped close to Samir. "If you're gonna kill me, nigga you better do it now because I promise you won't get a second chance." They stared daggers at each other. A gunshot went off from the second landing. When Samir looked to see who it was, Jamal hit him with a right hook. He grabbed his wrist, bending it back before lifting his arm up and punched him in the rib. He then snatched the gun and put Samir in a choke hold, shielding himself from his goons as they were now drawing their guns.

"Drop that shit!" Jamal yelled. He looked up in the direction where the gunshot came from but didn't see anyone. One of Samir's goons put his gun down but the other two remained defiant. Jamal noticed a red beam on one of their chests. He looked up in the direction it was coming from. D-Ball stepped from the shadows. Jamal had never been more happy to see him in his life.

"Put that shit away, homie. You already know I don't miss," D-Ball said with his voice echoing down below. He pulled his back-up gun and pointed it at the other gunman. They both dropped their weapons. "Kick that shit away," D-Ball ordered them. They complied and backed up as he made his way downstairs.

"You're playing a dangerous game, 'Mal." Samir warned.

"Who says I'm playing? You fucked up when you came after Keisha, her brother and her son. Keep thinking you're untouchable. Your punk-ass is about to get touched." Jamal put his knee in Samir's back and kicked him away making him stumble. He kept his gun aimed at him.

"You got the balls to threaten me, nigga?"

Jamal waited until D-Ball was next to him before unloading the clip and then taking Samir's gun apart. He stuck the clip in his coat pocket and dropped the pieces of the gun onto the floor. "I don't make threats; I make promises. And unlike you, I keep them." He walked over to where one of the guns were dropped and took the one that belonged to him while D-Ball covered him. They backed away towards the door so they could leave.

"This shit ain't over. Believe me when I say that. I'll be seeing both of you niggas again," Samir said in a menacing tone.

"I don't doubt that for one second," D-Ball said. He kept both of his guns aimed at Samir and his men while Jamal left out and then he left out behind him.

"How did you find me?" Jamal asked as he followed D-Ball to his car.

"The hospital released me and I was on my way home when I saw Samir sitting outside of your mom's house. I parked up the street and watched. When I saw you come out of Ms. Keyona's house and they took you, I followed y'all." D-Ball shook his head. "It was so tempting to kill that nigga right then and there." They climbed inside of his car. D-Ball rubbed his hand across the leg he had been shot in and took a deep breath.

"Who are you telling?" Jamal agreed. "I can't believe the hospital released you so quickly."

"Yeah, the bullet went in and out. No bones were damaged or none of that. They patched me up, gave me some meds, a prescription and sent me on my way. And it's a good thing too because Samir was about to get you the fuck outta here." He started the car and pulled off quickly. "You may not believe me but, Samir is scared of you. He's gotta be. Why else would he come after you just for coming back to Philly unless he thought you might come after him?"

Jamal thought about what D-Ball said as he played with the ring hanging around his neck. That had never occurred to him before. He figured Samir was doing it as a pre-caution because he knew too much.

He kissed the ring as he held it between his two fingers and then let it fall back against his chest. "I don't know," he mumbled.

"I heard what he said about your pop. Tell me he wasn't grimy enough to kill your old man, yo." D-Ball said.

"Yeah; killed him right in front of my mom back when me and Shawn were too young to remember him.

I found out back in high-school." Jamal shook his head as he thought back to that day. Anger was starting to consume him.

D-Ball shook his head as well. "See, that's the shit I don't like. That nigga has no loyalty to nobody. How he go all those years trying to groom you to be his soldier knowing he killed your pops? That nigga needs to be put down, ASAP." Jamal didn't say anything. "What are you still doing here anyway?" D-Ball asked.

"Unfinished business," Jamal replied. D-Ball didn't push the issue. He drove Jamal back to his mother's block so he could retrieve his car.

"Are you going to see Maurice?"

"Yeah, I have to make another stop though." Jamal thought about what was done to Keisha and debated whether or not he should tell D-Ball. "Ay listen; good looking out on backing me up back there. I really appreciate that, straight up. If you don't plan on leaving, I might need your help with something."

"What's up, homie?" D-Ball asked as he leaned into Jamal's car.

"The cop that was in your room last night, he wants me to help him take down Samir. I don't think he's one of the cops on Samir's payroll but I can't tell who else is. I would really appreciate it if I had someone at my back that I could trust; someone who wants to take Samir out as bad as I want to."

D-Ball thought for a moment. "Man, it's tempting as shit to put a bullet in that nigga. But after yesterday, I'm ready to just take all this shit as a loss and get the fuck outta dodge."

"I can dig that and I don't too much blame you. But just so you know, Samir sent a warning to Keisha by one of the cops he has working for him," Jamal said.

"Sent a warning like what?" D-Ball asked.

Jamal waited a moment before responding. He looked away and said, "Keisha was raped in her holding cell last night. The cop that did it beat her up pretty bad, too. She said he told her if her and Manny didn't leave, they would dump her body on her mother's door step."

D-Ball leaned back and looked at Jamal.

"That's why he said what he said about Keisha in that warehouse? Are you fucking kidding me!? He's that fucking grimy he had them fucking pigs do that shit to Manny's girl!?" D-Ball was more pissed than Jamal. He was ready to go back to the warehouse and blow Samir away at that very moment. Anger shook his body to the core.

"It was bad man, real bad. I wasn't going to stay; my plan was to leave this morning after I saw Maurice and my mom. But after that shit last night, enough is fucking enough. Too many good niggas are getting murked out here for his ass to still be kicking and breathing. I promise you, if I can't make the charges stick, I'ma kill that nigga myself for that shit," Jamal seethed.

"Not if I get to him first," D-Ball replied.

"If we're going to do this, we're doing this my way. After what just happened, we're both targets. But we can't be sloppy about this shit, you dig me?" Jamal said.

"I got you, homie." D-Ball nodded his head.

"I'm on my way to Davidson's crib. If you're in, follow me."

D-Ball hopped inside of his car and followed Jamal over to Keith Davidson's apartment.

17

Keisha stood outside of Maurice's room unseen but listening to her mother and Maurice talk. Thankfully they weren't talking about what happened that led to him being in the hospital with a bullet wound. She looked at Deisha who was expressionless.

Keisha couldn't tell who was more nervous; her or Deisha. "Are you going in?" Keisha asked Deisha.

Deisha rang her hands together. She took a deep breath after feeling like she hadn't taken a single one since they got onto the elevator. "You go in first," she said nervously. Deisha hadn't seen Maurice in over a year and wasn't sure if she was ready.

"Oh hell no! There is no way I'm facing him alone with my face like this. You said you would be with me every step of the way. Don't back out on me because of your own fears," Keisha hissed.

Deisha thought over what she said. She knew Keisha was right. She took a deep breath again and grabbed her by the hand so they could walk into Maurice's room together. Deisha's body shook all over and she was positive that she was visibly trembling. It was a love at first site moment for her as all of the feelings she had for him for more than ten years came back at that moment. Maurice stared at her and she stared back. He looked better than Deisha last remembered; his hair was still cut close and wavy as always but he had grown a goatee beard that was shaped up sharply and was attached to his side burns. She was speechless not because of how he looked or because he had been shot, but because she was staring the love of her life in his face and the feelings never diminished.

"Aren't you going to speak?" Maurice said to Deisha with a half-smile.

Deisha shook her head as if she were clearing it. "Hey," she said softly. "I can't believe you were shot…"

Maurice shrugged his shoulders as if it didn't matter. "I'm still here though."

"I'm glad," Deisha said. She had been trying to suppress her smile but at that moment, she failed. She blushed more than she anticipated.

Maurice chuckled and then looked at Keisha. His smile faded when he noticed the glasses. "What's up with the shades, Keesh? You're in your Stevie Wonder bag right now?" he joked.

Keisha touched them nervously. "No, I just have a headache and was trying to block out the light." She looked at her mother who was looking at her strangely.

"Keisha, take the sunglasses off, now," Ms. Brown said sternly. Keisha tried to protest but Ms. Brown put her hand up to silence her. "I said take them off. It wasn't a request."

Keisha took the glasses off slowly and looked at the floor. Maurice struggled to sit up in his bed so he could look at her. The room held the kind of silence that was deafening to all occupants of his hospital room.

Ms. Brown cleared her throat deciding to break the silence. "Keisha told me that some chicken-head came up to the hospital claiming to have been in a relationship with Manny for six months. They got into a scuffle and that's why her face looks like that."

Keisha looked at Maurice. He could tell by the look in her eyes that she was begging him not to debunk that lie. Maurice looked at Deisha and then looked at his mother.

"Mom, I'm hungry and I really don't want to eat this hospital food. I heard there's a Pei Wei's not too far from here. Can you hook me up?" Maurice asked as he stared at Keisha.

"Right now?" Ms. Brown asked as she looked at her son and then her daughter.

"Yes mom, I'm hungrier than a mug," Maurice said as he rubbed his stomach to drive the point home.

Ms. Brown grabbed her coat and put it on before getting her purse. "I don't know what's going on, but I raised y'all and I know when something is up. You have 30 minutes to say whatever it is you want to say without me around." She left the room and closed the door behind her. Maurice fixed his eyes on Keisha. She bit her bottom lip and looked at the floor to avoid eye contact.

"Keisha," Maurice called to his sister. "Say something, because what you told mommy was a straight fucking lie! I was with you from the time you got to the hospital until the time we got ambushed at your apartment. What the fuck happened afterwards?"

Keisha turned her back and put her hands to her face. She breathed heavily as she tried to gather the courage to speak.

"Keisha," Deisha started. Keisha shook her head with her hands to her face as she cried.

"Keisha!" Maurice said, raising his voice.

"Got damn it!" Keisha said before crying louder. She wiped her face and looked at Deisha. "I can't tell this story again."

Deisha looked at Keisha and then looked at Maurice. "Keisha killed one of the gunmen that came after y'all at the apartment."

"Yeah, I know that." Maurice said as he looked at Deisha.

Deisha took a deep breath and closed her eyes. "She was taken into custody right after you went into surgery. They left her in a holding cell for two hours and didn't allow her to make a phone call. A cop came in and told her that she was going to be released…" Deisha trailed off. She couldn't open her eyes. She didn't want to see the expression on Maurice's face when she told him that his sister had been brutally raped by a cop and the brutal rape was ordered by Samir. She gave a detailed account just as Keisha did when they were in the back of Jamal's car coming back to her condo. When she finished, she kept her eyes closed for a moment, afraid to look at Maurice. She finally opened them and was shocked to see Maurice with his hands over his face in tears.

He breathed heavily trying his best not to let his anger consume him but it was quickly turning into rage. He wiped his face and took a deep breath. "I'm going to fucking kill him," Maurice said in a shaky voice.

Keisha finally looked at her brother. He motioned for her to come to him and she did. She climbed in his hospital bed and he held her as she cried. Maurice looked up at Deisha. She wiped her eyes and mouthed, "I'm sorry." The only thing Maurice could do was shake his head.

Maurice was at a loss for words. He never imagined that they would be in the position that they were in at that very moment; his little sister killed a man and was brutally raped the same day that he had been shot along with her boyfriend and her boyfriend's brother. How much pain was she to endure in such a short amount of time?

18

Jamal pulled up to the Regency Apartment complex and called Detective Davidson from his car. Davidson told him what apartment to come to and buzzed him up. D-Ball followed behind. Davidson let Jamal in shocked to see D-Ball with him.

"I was expecting you to be alone," Davidson said as he looked at D-Ball. "The hospital released you already?"

"Yeah, you know hospitals don't really keep people like that no more unless they can find other ways to milk your insurance." D-Ball hobbled over to a sofa and sat down, wincing in pain. He reached in his coat pocket and pulled out a bottle of pills that the hospital prescribed to him. He popped two in his mouth and swallowed them down without water before leaning his head against the back of the sofa and closing his eyes.

"Samir came for me," Jamal told Davidson as he pulled his gun from his back and sat it on the counter.

"Wait, what do you mean Samir came for you; today?" Davidson asked as he looked at Jamal seriously.

"Yeah, I saw him waiting outside of Ms. Keyona's house. When Jamal came out, they made him get in a car and I followed them." D-Ball replied, still leaning back on the couch with his eyes closed.

"And if it wasn't for D-Ball, I'd probably be dead right now," Jamal chimed in.

"I don't understand. Why would Samir come after you, Jamal? You just came to the city yesterday and haven't done much." Davidson was confused.

"That's because his bitch-ass is too scared that Jamal might actually come after his ass this time," D-Ball answered.

"Actually, I think it's that along with the fact that I probably was seen with you," Jamal said. He looked at Davidson. "What exactly is it that you wanted me to do?"

"Does this mean you'll help me?" Davidson asked with a hopeful expression on his face.

Jamal hesitated for a brief moment before answering. "I don't think I have much of a choice now," he said with a sigh. "After what just happened, I would bet money that Samir is plotting on how he can take me out without it looking too suspicious. The fact that I'm a detective with the DPD doesn't faze him. It wouldn't matter if I was killed there or in Philly. He could make it look like a situation where I was at the wrong place at the wrong time, a robbery or whatever."

"Well that's good to know," Davidson said with a smile. "But tell me something; if Samir didn't come after you today, would you have been willing to help? Or would you have gone back to Delaware without a care in the world?"

"It was what they did to Keisha that made me realize I needed to stay," Jamal replied.

"What do you mean? What did they do to Keisha?"

Jamal looked at Davidson and shook his head. "A cop raped her and beat the shit outta her in her holding cell last night before they released her."

"Get the fuck outta here!" Davidson piped. "Where is Keisha now?"

"Deisha just texted me and told me they're at the hospital visiting Maurice. He knows and he is pissed."

"I know damn well he is!" Davidson shook his head. "Samir needs his ass busted immediately. He needs to be put away for life."

"Nah, somebody should've killed his ass a long muthafucking time ago," D-Ball said as he looked up.

"Fucking right on that shit. An animal like that you can't just send to prison. He has too much pull and it ain't no telling how far it goes. He needs to be put down not put away," Jamal agreed.

"As far as I can tell after going over some stuff, he might have pull as high up as IAB," Davidson said. He pulled out a box of pizza from the night before. "Y'all hungry?"

"Nah, I'm good," Jamal said as he waved his hand.

"What you got over there? Ain't no swine, is it?" D-Ball asked.

"Nah, it's garlic and chicken pizza from Papa Johns," Davidson replied as he opened the box so D-Ball could see.

"Yeah, let me get down with some of that. Temple got some nasty ass food and I'm hungry as shit right now," D-Ball replied.

"You ain't never lied about that shit," Jamal chuckled. Davidson put the left over pizza in a pan and placed it in his oven. "So what makes you think Samir has IAB on his payroll?" Jamal asked Davidson.

"Well, there was a raid on an IAB transfer back in 2002. Guns and drugs were confiscated and two federal officers were killed. The IAB officer in charge of the security detail was an Alekzander Kristoff."

Jamal shook his head. "His fucking name just keeps coming up."

"You heard of him?" Davidson asked him.

Jamal looked at Davidson for a moment. He was trying to figure out how much he should tell this cop and if he could be trusted. It didn't matter at this point. Jamal knew Davidson was piecing together his past. He had two options; help Davidson put Samir away and pray that he wasn't next on his list to take down, or go back to Delaware as if the last 24 hours had not happened with Samir after him as well as the cops if Davidson opened his mouth about what he knew. He was not trying to bring his problems home.

Jamal let out a deep sigh and said, "Kristoff was with Samir the night he killed my father. I didn't find out he was a cop until I talked to D-Ball yesterday before you came in."

Davidson was about to take a sip of his coffee and stopped. He looked over at Jamal for a space of heartbeats as he tried to grasp what he had just been told. Now he knew where the connection was coming from. "Let me make sure I understand what you just said. Samir killed your father and Kristoff was there when he did it. When the hell did this happen?"

"From what my mom told me, way back in '87."

Davidson shook his head and began thinking. This shit was too much for his mind to process. There were dirty cops on the force all the way back to the 80's.

"Okay, I need to know what you know about Kristoff."

"Listen," Jamal started. "I'm not trying to be giving up information and letting skeletons out the closet only for the shit to fall back on me once this is all over with. If I help you, I want my file destroyed; permanently. I don't want anyone else to be able to go sniffing around my fucking past. I know I fucked up as a kid. I didn't know any better. I could partially blame that on the fact that my mother kept this shit about Samir killing my father from me for almost 15 fucking years. But at the end of the day, I made my own decisions. But I think I've more than paid for the shit I did. I made a life for myself. If I can close this chapter of my life by finally getting Samir out of the way, then great. But I am NOT going back to jail. Not for you," Jamal said as he looked Davidson in the eye, "not for nobody."

Davidson waited a moment to make sure Jamal was finished his tirade before he spoke. "Jamal, I told you yesterday, I'm not after you. I never intended to come after you. I needed some background information, that's all."

"Basically he was going to blackmail you into helping him by threatening to expose your file," D-Ball said as he looked at Davidson with cold eyes. "That's fucked up."

"Yeah I know. Not a smart move to make because what's in my file can be connected to Samir which can be connected to whatever dirty cop is on the force. They would take you out before you had a chance," Jamal replied.

"Yup, just like Parker. Pay attention, cop. Everybody is expendable and these niggas ain't leaving no loose ends." D-Ball said.

Davidson hadn't looked at it that way. He was so focused on the possibility of getting rid of Samir that he didn't factor in the possibility that he could be putting a target on his back. He shook his head. "Jamal, you have my word that anything I figured out or anything that you've told me, I promise you that it will not go any further than this room."

"That's not good enough." Jamal said as he shook his head. "This muthafucka is coming after me now. I want my file deleted. I want immunity; period." Jamal said firmly. "If I can't get that, then we've got no deal."

Davidson thought for a moment. "I can swing that. You have my word." They were all quiet as Davidson took the pizza out of his oven and gave some to D-Ball. Jamal changed his mind and took a slice also.

"I still need to know what you know about Kristoff and how he's connected to your father. Tell me what happened."

Jamal took a bite of his slice of pizza and thought back to the night in his mother's bedroom when he found out the shocking truth behind what really happened to his father. It had dawned on him at that moment that he was so focused on leaving his past behind that he never even looked into his father's records. He never checked to see if he could get any information on him. He told the story of his father's murder to Davidson and D-Ball the way it had been told to him ten years prior.

"I don't even remember him. All those years, I thought my father was the typical dead beat dad that just left my mom struggling to take care of me and my brother. I didn't know until then that Samir had my mom living in fear. But the damage had already been done."

"You mean Khalil?" Davidson asked as he sipped his coffee. He studied Jamal's face to gauge his reaction. Jamal stared back and dropped his eyes.

"If I had known what Samir had done, I never would've went to him."

"No, you would've tried to do it yourself and your ass would either be dead or in jail," Davidson replied.

Jamal had no argument for what Davidson said because he knew he was right. In the long run, Jamal still ended up on the losing end of the gamble and now thirteen years later, he was right back where he was before; at the mercy of Samir.

19

Keisha left Maurice's hospital room with their mother so she could get Kamir. Deisha was going to leave also but Maurice convinced her to stay behind. She wasn't sure what she was going to say to him. They hadn't spoken in over a year due to Deisha getting an abortion behind Maurice's back and turning down his marriage proposal. She didn't turn him down because she didn't want to be his wife. Deisha was afraid of becoming a carbon copy of her mother more than anything in the world and didn't think that she was wife material. Her childhood had left her damaged; an over achiever trying hard to prove that she was different from her mother.

Maurice was furious when he learned that Deisha aborted his child behind his back. She didn't give him an option and what was even more hurtful was the fact that Deisha had turned him down when he asked her to be his wife. They had made it through so much, but that was unforgiveable in his eyes. To him, Deisha was afraid of commitment, selfish and self-absorbed in a hell that had ended long ago.

He stared at her for a long time before finally saying something. "How have you been?"

"I've been good," Deisha replied nervously. She began ringing her hands together again. Maurice looked at her and smiled.

"I see old habits die hard," Maurice said with a grin.

"What do you mean?" she asked.

Maurice pointed to her hands. "You ring your hands when you're nervous. You pull the bottom of your shirt or jacket when you're scared." Deisha noticed she was about to pull the bottom of her leather jacket and stopped. Instead, she put her hand behind her back. Maurice smiled at her again and shook his head.

"What about you? How have you been?" Deisha asked back.

"Oh you know; same o-same-o. But I figured I'd break up the monotony and get a cap busted in my ass," he joked, trying to make light of the situation.

Deisha chuckled. She caught the way he was staring at her and started ringing her hands together again. "Stop that," Maurice said.

"I can't help it," Deisha laughed.

"Do I make you nervous?"

Deisha hesitated for a moment. "No, don't be ridiculous."

They fell silent for a moment. Deisha couldn't take the way Maurice was staring at her, almost as if he was studying her. She looked out of the window to avoid his glare.

"Can I ask you a question?" Maurice asked.

"Sure."

"Why did you change your mind and gave me back the ring?" Maurice asked.

Deisha had a feeling that question was coming. She closed her eyes and took a deep breath. "It wasn't you, Maurice. It was me," she started.

Maurice interrupted her. "Please don't give me that "it's not you, it's me" bullshit. I'm better than that."

"No Maurice, listen. I spent my teenage years and my twenties working so hard to make sure I didn't end up like my mom. That has always been my biggest fear. That's why I studied so hard, that's why I always pushed myself with everything I did. I wanted to say yes. I didn't change my mind because I didn't want to marry you. I was just scared that I couldn't keep you. I'm scared of being a shitty mom like mines was." She stopped talking but kept her eyes closed.

"Look at me, Deisha." Maurice said to her. Deisha waited a moment before doing as he asked. She did her best to make eye contact with him. "You can't be afraid of failure because you can't always get everything right.

You're not perfect. I never wanted you to be perfect. I loved you for you, flaws and all. You were scared you couldn't keep me? You kept me for twelve years. In my eyes, you were already my wife; I just wanted to make it official. But you keep running from me. I'm not gonna hurt you. I never would."

Deisha couldn't meet his gaze anymore and looked at the floor. "But I hurt you," she said in a soft voice. "What I did…"

Maurice shushed her. "I don't want to talk about that," he said interrupting her.

"I'm sorry… I'm so sorry, Maurice." Deisha said sorrowfully.

Maurice shook his head. "Don't, Deisha."

They fell silent for a moment. So many thoughts were running through Deisha's mind. There was so much that she wanted to say but didn't know where to start. She waited a moment and then finally blurted out. "Do you still love me?"

Maurice looked at her for a moment. They had been separated for a year. That was the longest they had ever been away from each other. In that year he mostly focused on work. Females flocked to him, flirted with him and even asked him out on dates. But his heart was still with Deisha.

"I never stopped," he replied as he stared at her. "And you?"

"I never stopped either," Deisha said in return. Maurice motioned for her to come to him with his finger. When she came to him, he pulled her onto his hospital bed by her waist and kissed her. Deisha put her hands to his face and exhaled. She had waited for this moment for a year but it felt like forever. She looked him in his eyes and kissed him back. "I missed you."

"I missed you, too." Maurice said as he moved her hair behind her ear.

"I love you." Deisha said as she leaned her forehead against his.

"I love you, too."

Deisha closed her eyes and shook her head. One year had been too long. She feared for so long that Maurice would never forgive her or speak to her again. She thought back to what Jamal said to her the night before and realized he was right. She needed to trust in her man and believe he would always be there for her. They kissed each other longingly until they heard somebody whistle from the doorway and clap.

"Yeah!" Jamal said as he clapped his hands together. "It's about got-damn time, yo."

Deisha looked at Jamal and laughed before burying her face in Maurice's shoulder to hide the fact that she was blushing.

D-Ball laughed with Jamal as they came inside. "I would say get a room, but you niggas already in one."

They all laughed together. D-Ball walked to Maurice's bed and shook his hand. He gave Deisha a half hug. Jamal shook Maurice's hand also.

"Good looking back at Keisha's apartment," Maurice said to D-Ball.

"No problem, homie. I'd do that shit again in a heartbeat, no questions asked," D-Ball said as he sat in a chair.

"So y'all two back together?" Jamal asked.

Maurice looked at Deisha. "I don't know. Are we?"

Deisha nodded. "I'm not going anywhere. You're going somewhere?"

"Nah babe, you're stuck with me." Maurice kissed her forehead and pulled Deisha close to him.

Jamal smiled at them. "That's what's up."

"I thought you would've rolled out by now, 'Mal." Maurice said.

"Yeah, I should've but there's some shit I need to handle before I can go back home." Jamal stood in front of the window with his arm up, leaning into the glass. He looked down below at the people moving about before closing his eyes. "Deisha told me you know about Keisha."

"I know that's your cousin, Jamal. But Keisha is my sister. Don't nobody put their hands on my muthafucking sister and live to talk about that shit. I wanna body that nigga so bad, yo."

"Who you fucking telling?" D-Ball said as he shook his head. "I'm so fucking pissed over that shit."

"I owe no loyalties to Samir. That shit stopped when I found out he killed my fucking father. What he did to Keisha was outta pocket, straight up." Jamal said calmly.

"So what are you going to do about it?" Maurice asked.

Jamal turned around and looked at Maurice and Deisha. He stared at Deisha for a while. "You wanna hear this, Deisha?"

"I don't think it's anything I can't handle," she replied.

Jamal waited a moment before speaking again. "There's a cop that's been piecing together some things. He knows there are dirty cops on the force that are working for Samir. Samir has protection all the way up to IAB. Now he wants to try to take Samir down, but by the book. That shit ain't happening."

"So what are you saying?" Maurice asked, waiting for the other shoe to drop.

"He wants me to help him bring Samir down. But I need somebody that's got my back. I ain't trusting the fucking Philly Pigs because I don't know who's on Samir's team and who ain't."

"Say no more. I got you," Maurice said. He slapped Jamal a handshake.

"Wait, are you serious?" Deisha asked as she sat up and looked at Jamal and Maurice. "You've just been shot, Maurice. Why are you trying to get into some shit like this?"

"Deisha, this nigga tried to kill me and my sister. He had a punk-ass cop rape my sister. His ass got to fucking go, ASAP. Fuck that," Maurice replied acidly.

"But…" Deisha started.

"Ain't no buts, babe. Who's to say he won't come after me again? 'Mal just said he got police protection so trying to do this shit the legal way ain't gonna fucking fly!"

"Yeah, Davidson needs to get on board. These fucking pigs are killing each other to keep shit quiet.

They def won't have a problem knocking us the fuck off," D-Ball chimed in.

"Yeah and they already came for me today when I was coming from my mom's house. If it weren't for D-Ball, my ass would be outta here," Jamal said.

Deisha looked at Maurice and then Jamal. "I lost Tamera. Kiree is dead, too. I don't wanna have to bury y'all."

"Deisha, if we don't go after him, he's coming after us. This shit just turned into kill or be killed. They came after me and Keisha last night. That's the fuck why I'm in here now. He won't get a second chance. Fuck that. I'm on this shit. Just let me know what I need to do."

Deisha closed her eyes. She then looked at D-Ball. "You too?" she asked.

D-Ball looked at her with a smirk on his face. "If I get to be the one to pull the trigger, it's all love."

Deisha then remembered something. "Manny doesn't know."

"He doesn't know what?" Jamal asked.

"What happened to Keisha; he doesn't even know his mom passed away. Keisha won't tell him because he's so weak. She's trying to wait for him to get stronger before she tells him."

"You can't be fucking serious," Maurice said.

"Yo, when Manny finds out, he's gonna go fucking nuts." D-Ball shook his head. "His brother, his mom and then Samir had that shit done to Keisha? Man, it's gonna take like five of us to hold him back."

"Somebody needs to tell him," Jamal said.

"Keisha needs to be the one to tell him," Maurice said. "And she needs to tell him soon because we might need him."

"Ain't no might about it. We will need him." Jamal replied. "Me and D-Ball are the targets. Samir ain't worried about you or Manny. Let's keep it that way until Manny is better."

"What about the cop?" D-Ball asked.

Jamal looked at him and smirked. "Accidents happen. Bottom line is Philly will be a lot safer with Samir dead, not in jail."

D-Ball agreed. Jamal looked back out of the window again as he began to play with the ring that hung from his neck. He prayed that for once, things went according to plan. He desperately wanted this chapter of his life to close permanently without losing anymore of the people he loved. He kissed Tamera's ring and tucked it back inside of his shirt.

20

Keisha convinced her mother to keep her son Kamir for her. Jamal and D-Ball took her back to her apartment and she retrieved the money and keys to the house in Glenolden. She packed up as much of their things that she could carry in both of their cars with the hope that she would be able to come back later on and get the rest. As a precaution, D-Ball stayed at the house with her so she didn't have to be there alone.

Davidson worked out a deal with the Delaware Police Department and had Jamal temporarily assigned to the Philadelphia Police Department. Samir found out about it and became irate. He was hoping that his cousin would simply go back to Delaware. With Jamal still in Philly and assigned to the PPD, he had to change his entire approach. Jamal had to die, but he had to do it in a way that either looked like an accident or a drug bust gone wrong. He pulled the heat off of Jamal to make him think that everything was fine. But Jamal knew better. He was not going to drop his guard.

After a week in the hospital, Manny was doing much better. His recovery was happening a little faster than anyone anticipated. He was up and moving around on his own, a bit. No blood clots had formed and he was expected to return home soon. Keisha was unable to keep up with the lies and she had no choice but to tell him that his mother passed away. Manny was furiously hysterical. He punched a hole in the wall of his hospital room and refused to let Keisha touch him. She backed away into a corner in part fear and in part sorrow as Manny trashed his hospital room. Security and nurses came in. A security guard was about to handcuff him but Keisha quickly explained that he had just learned that his mother had passed away. She went to Manny and pleaded with him to calm down. The loss of his brother and his mother broke his heart. He collapsed in Keisha's arms and cried like a baby. She waved for security and the nurses to leave his room promising she would clean everything up once he settled down.

After seeing Manny's reaction to his mother's passing, she decided to wait a little longer to tell him about the rape. In the back of her mind, she was praying that she didn't have to tell him at all. She was still having a hard time processing what happened. The dark frightened her so she slept with the lights on. Keisha was dealing with her assault the wrong way by pretending it didn't happen and trying her best not to think about it. Sometimes, the slightest movement or coming across a man who wore Old Spice gave her flashes from that night, making her re-live that horrible moment.

Manny couldn't believe that he would be burying his brother and his mother. Emotionally, he was in no position to make decisions for the services for either of them, so Keisha took on that task as well. Keisha kept herself busy with making the arrangements for the candle light vigil as well as the funeral for both Kiree and Ms. Becky while Manny finished out his last days in the hospital. They decided to make it a double funeral so Manny did not have to suffer through two separate services.

Keisha spent the entire Friday picking up the obituaries for Ms. Becky and Kiree as well as the cards to inform every one of the funeral that would be held that Monday for the both of them. After handing them out to the people from the neighborhood and making sure everything was in order for the candle light vigil for both Kiree and Ms. Becky that Saturday evening, she went straight back to the house in Glenolden.

D-Ball was sitting in the living room waiting for her. He was cleaning one of his guns and watching a basketball game on TV when she came in. She sat on the couch next to him and put her hands to her face.

She was exhausted physically and mentally and emotionally drained.

D-Ball looked at her. "Are you okay?"

Keisha waited a moment before answering. "I'm so tired," she said in a shaky voice. "I'm trying to hold it together for Manny and for my son, but got-damn it I am so tired."

"You haven't had a chance to just sit down. You're trying to keep busy to make sure you don't have to think about what happened these last couple weeks." D-Ball said as he loaded bullets into a clip.

"Can you blame me?" Keisha replied.

"Not at all. But I'ma tell you; when this funeral is over, when you finish cleaning dishes, when the people are gone and you actually sit down and the silence starts to surround you, that shit is gonna hit like a ton of bricks."

"I'm not looking forward to that at all," Keisha said as she sighed. "Did you eat?"

"Nah."

"Well, I'm about to make some Quesadillas. You down?"

"Hell yeah. Just make sure you don't put any swine in there," D-Ball laughed. Keisha laughed with him and went into the kitchen to wash her hands. She cooked dinner and they ate and talked until late that night when D-Ball decided to go to the guest room and turn in.

Keisha showered and then went to her room to head to bed as well. Manny was being released from the hospital early in the morning and she wanted to be the one to pick him up with Kamir and bring them back to their new home. She thought she wasn't going to like the new house over the apartment that they shared for almost four years but the house was gorgeous and in a suburban neighborhood. They had a two car garage with a basement, three bedrooms, a den, an eat in kitchen, big beautiful bay windows in the living room that let in lots of sunlight, and a front and a back porch with an old fashioned swing. Though there was furniture moderately placed about, Keisha couldn't wait to really get in there and start decorating.

Keisha went into the bedroom and began getting ready for bed. She stared at herself in the mirror after putting on Manny's tee-shirt to sleep in. Though the bruises on her face had completely healed, the scars from the rape were still there. She shook her head, forcing herself not to think about it and wrapped her hair before climbing into the bed. After what she endured at the police station, Keisha no longer slept with the light off and kept a .22 pistol under a pillow next to her. She pulled her comforter up close to her face and before she knew it, she drifted off to sleep.

She had barely been sleeping for an hour when she began to toss and turn. The memory of the rape was coming back to her. She could see the cop so clearly; the wicked smirk on his face, his empty and emotionless eyes. What was worse was she could smell his Old Spice cologne. It was strong and distinct; very strong. Keisha opened her eyes and was shocked that she was in the dark. She lay frozen in her bed with her heart racing. She left the light on. She knew she left the light on. Did D-Ball turn her light off after possibly checking in on her before going to sleep? No, because she had already forewarned him of her fear of the dark.

Maybe the bulb blew out. Keisha was quickly becoming overwhelmed with fear as her eyes searched wildly in the dark. She tried to remind herself to breathe as her heart raced and beat so loudly she was positive she could hear it. She breathed in and then breathed out. She breathed in again and that's when she noticed it; the smell of the Old Spice Cologne wasn't distinct because her dream had felt so real. The smell was distinct because somebody was in her room. Just as she tried to jump up she felt a strong hand go over her mouth muffling her before she had the chance to scream. The same sonuva bitch cop from the precinct was in her house, in her room, in her bed and trying to strong arm her again.

Keisha panicked. She wondered how the cop had found her and how he had gotten into her house. She also wondered if Samir had sent him again and if something had been done to D-Ball. The cop pushed her back onto the bed with his hand over her mouth. She felt his hand fondling her again as he had done in the precinct. She was in fear and trembling as she lay frozen. When she felt him lick the side of her face again like he had done previously, she snapped. This shit was not about to happen again.

Keisha struggled against him, causing his hand to slide down her mouth just enough for her to bite him. She sank her teeth into the side of his hand as hard as she could. Reflex caused him to snatch his hand away and she screamed for D-Ball as loud as she could. The cop punched her as he did in her holding cell, but Keisha didn't back down. She grabbed him by his head and head butt him as hard as she could, damn near causing herself to black out. He fell back and Keisha tried to scramble from the bed but was tangled in her sheets.

The bedroom door knob jiggled but it was locked.

"Keisha!" D-Ball yelled from the other side.

The cop wasn't aware that anyone was in the house with her. Keisha had fallen from the bed to the floor and was trying to crawl away but the cop snatched her by her hair. She screamed for D-Ball again, pleading for him to help her.

The cop snatched her up by her hair and back slapped her. "You bitch!" he scowled. She fell backwards into the night stand, knocking over the lamp. After falling to the floor she heard the cop coming for her again. She grabbed the lamp and swung at him as hard as she could, hoping that she caught him in the head, but she only hit his shoulder. The hit was strong enough to make him stagger back giving her only a moment to act fast. She got up and scrambled to her bed grabbing her gun from under the pillow, screaming. She turned over on her back as fast as she could and fired five shots hitting the cop in his upper torso. He dropped to the floor and didn't move.

D-Ball had been outside of the room ramming on the door with his shoulder trying to break it down. He had just run back to his room to get his gun when he heard the gunshots. His heart raced, praying that he wasn't too late. He aimed at Keisha's door waiting to hear movement. He started to shoot the lock off but instead he kicked the door with everything he had. The side panel's wood split and the door gave way. He saw Keisha sitting against the head board still holding her gun with both of her hands, aiming it at the cop on the floor. D-Ball looked at the cop and then looked at Keisha. She had a look of horror on her face and was trembling. The corner of her mouth was bloody and her room was a mess.

"Keisha," D-Ball called to her. Keisha didn't hear him. It was almost as if she were in a trance. D-Ball turned on the ceiling light and walked over to her. He put his hand over hers, making her lower the gun. "It's okay, Keesh. Gimme the gun."

Keisha looked up at him as he eased the gun from her hands. "Is he dead?" she asked in a shaky voice.

"I didn't check," D-Ball said as he grabbed her phone that was knocked to the floor during the scuffle.

"He was going to rape me again," she said. She put her hands to her face and closed her eyes, beginning to rock back and forth. D-Ball dialed 9-11.

"Yes, I want to report a break-in and attempted rape," D-Ball said to the operator. He watched Keisha as she rocked herself while he told the operator that the attacker was shot but he did not know if he was still alive. He answered the operator's questions and then gave the address. When he disconnected the call he looked at Keisha. She was still rocking back and forth on the bed. He then made a call to Jamal and Maurice. They both said they would be there as soon as they could.

D-Ball reached out to rub Keisha's back and she jumped. "Keisha…" D-Ball started to say but couldn't find the words. He could only imagine what she was going through with the possibility that she had killed another man in less than two weeks and was almost raped again. He heard the sirens and went downstairs to wait for the police. When they arrived, he led them upstairs. A few of the cops spoke with D-Ball and he explained what he knew as far as being awakened from his sleep because he heard Keisha screaming for him to help her. A couple of cops checked the front door and saw there was no forced entry but the back door appeared to have been jimmied.

Though D-Ball didn't particularly care for cops, he cooperated for the sake of Keisha. He gave his full name and surrendered his driver's license and gun permit. He was surprised at how understanding the police were to him.

There were detectives in Keisha's room taking pictures and interviewing her. Her attacker was still alive and was being loaded into an ambulance and taken to a nearby hospital.

"I went to bed with my light on. I sleep with my light on because I'm scared of the dark now," Keisha explained in a shaky voice. "I woke up because I smelled Old Spice. At first I thought it was my dream but it wasn't. When I woke up, I noticed my room was dark but I didn't turn my light off. I tried to get up but he put his hand over my mouth to keep me from screaming. He started touching me," Keisha described with a shaky hand, rubbing it on the side of her face that was licked and punched. "He licked the side of my face just like before…"

"What do you mean just like before? Did you know your attacker?" one of the detectives asked.

D-Ball was standing in the doorway looking down at her. "Tell him, Keisha. You have to tell them."

"Ma'm?" the detective asked.

"They won't believe me," Keisha said to D-Ball with tears in her eyes.

"Ma'm, if this man attacked you before, you need to let us know. We can help you and make sure he doesn't do this to another woman again," the cop assured her.

Keisha smirked sarcastically and shook her head. She ignored the question and finished explaining what happened in her bedroom instead.

"Okay," the cop said as he finished jotting down his notes. "We were able to see that the back door had been tampered with. Apparently that was his point of entry and then he used the stairs in the kitchen to make his way up here to your room. We will need to take you down to the station to get an official statement from you."

Keisha nodded. She reached in the dresser drawer and grabbed a pair of sweat pants and a pair of socks to put on with her sneakers. She ran her fingers through her hair, smoothing it to the back as best as she could. As she was leaving the room she saw the blood on the floor and froze.

"Ms. Brown?" the cop called to her. Keisha was unresponsive, still looking at the blood on the carpet. "Ms. Brown?" the cop said again.

Keisha shook her head quickly and then looked at him as if she had been snapped out of a trance. She followed the cop downstairs.

"I'ma stay here until Jamal and Maurice comes, unless you want me to come with you?" D-Ball asked.

"No, wait for Jamal and Maurice," Keisha told him. She left with the cop and let him take her to the police station.

D-Ball stayed out of the way as the cops finished their investigation. Moments after Keisha left, Jamal and Maurice pulled up with Deisha riding with Maurice. Deisha jumped from the car before it came to a complete stop. She hadn't heard the entire story but was scared out of her mind once she saw the cops and yellow tape outside of the house. A cop grabbed her.

"Ma'm you can't go in there," the cop said to her. Maurice and Jamal followed behind her. Jamal flashed his badge.

"This is my sister's house; Keisha Brown. I got a call that she was attacked and shot someone," Maurice said.

"She's been taken to the police station to make a formal statement," the cop explained. Once the cops were finished their investigation, he stepped aside and let them in the house. D-Ball was in the kitchen leaning on the counter.

"What the hell happened, D-Ball?" Maurice asked.

"I don't know. Keisha went to bed. I went to bed right after her. Next thing you know, I hear her screaming for me to help her. I tried to get in her room but it was locked from the inside. I could hear shit crashing in there like she was fighting somebody. When I ran to get my gun, I heard the gunshots and it got quiet. I kicked the door in and she was just sitting on the bed, aiming the gun." D-Ball explained.

"Was it the same guy?" Deisha asked.

"She said it was."

"How the fuck did he find her?" Jamal seethed.

"I don't know." D-Ball shrugged.

Maurice thought for a moment. "Me and Keisha were leaving the hospital the other day and she said she thought she saw someone but she never said who. But she looked scared, I mean fucking terrified. I thought maybe she was still shook up from everything that's been going on."

"She saw him," Deisha said. "That sick sonuva bitch was following her."

Jamal shook his head. "This is bad man, this is real bad."

"What do you mean?" Maurice asked.

"Keisha just caught a body a couple of weeks ago. Now she's shooting someone else?" Jamal replied.

"Because of your sick fucking cousin!" Maurice snapped. "What the fuck was she supposed to do; let him rape her again?"

Deisha rubbed his back. "Babe, calm down."

Maurice took a deep breath and hung his head as he tried to calm down. He didn't mean to take his anger out on Jamal but he was pissed and did not like the idea of his sister being attacked again.

Jamal knew Maurice was upset and he had a right to be. All of this had transpired because Samir had been allowed to wreak havoc for so long. He took a deep breath before responding. "I don't disagree with you. But what I'm trying to tell you is they are going to question how Keisha got caught up in two separate shootings in two separate places of residence. I can back her up on the first one. And maybe D-Ball will be able to back her up on this one. But it would've helped if Keisha had reported that rape."

Maurice shook his head. He wanted Samir dead more than anything in the world. He went upstairs to his sister's bedroom. Deisha, Jamal and D-Ball followed behind. Maurice looked around the room and shook his head in disgust.

"I need to get to the police station to make sure she's okay," Maurice said. He looked around for a little while longer before going back downstairs and out to his car. He and Deisha jumped into his car and pulled off with Jamal following behind D-Ball's car.

The police made them sit in the lobby as Keisha was still making her statement. It went from her giving a detailed account of what happened, to excessive questioning once they found out her accuser was a cop as well as the fact that she had shot and killed another man in a similar situation a little more than a week prior to this incident. Keisha was trying hard not to speak on what happened in her holding cell but one of the cops could tell something was missing from her story.

"Ms. Brown, maybe Officer O'Brien lives a secret life as a rapist. Stranger things have happened. But that still doesn't explain why he would pick you? Why would he travel from his residence in Jenkintown all the way out near the airport to your home? What aren't you telling us?" the female officer asked.

Keisha was becoming angry at how they were turning this around as if she was the one at fault and he was innocent.

"Why does it feel like y'all are turning this shit around like this is my fault? He was in MY house! Look at my got-damn face! This is nothing compared to what he did to me last time. Yes! YES! Last time! Almost two weeks ago, that sick fuck raped me in my holding cell in Jenkintown. That's how he was able to just pick me! I was attacked and nearly killed in MY HOME! My son, my brother; all of us could have been killed if I didn't do what I did. And that sonuva bitch raped me and beat me up and told me if I told anyone he would dump my body on my mother's door step!"

Keisha was furious and in tears. She buried her face in her hands and wept helplessly. All of the pain, anger, hurt, and sorrow that she had been holding in calling herself being strong finally became too much for her to bare and came crashing down like a house made out of a deck of cards that had met a brisk breeze. She wept for Kiree, she wept for Ms. Becky. She wept for her son and for her brother and for Manny. She let out gut wrenching, shoulder shaking sobs.

The female officer signaled for her partner to leave the room they were in and then sat next to Keisha. She handed her a tissue and rubbed her back.

"Ms. Brown?" the female officer said once it began to sound like Keisha was calming down. "Why didn't you report it?"

"Because he's a cop," Keisha said as she looked at her through tear drenched eyes. "Because he's a cop and someone already tried to kill me once. I wasn't about to give them a second chance. Who would have believed me if I told them a cop raped me? Hell, as loud as I was screaming in that holding cell yet nobody came to see what was going on tells me I'm not the only one!" Keisha wiped her eyes and took a deep breath. "He did take a souvenir though."

"What was that?" the female officer asked.

"He tore my panties off. I remember when I was laying on the floor I saw when he tucked them in his back pocket. Maybe he didn't throw them away," she told her.

The officer looked at Keisha for a moment and then told her she would be right back. It seemed like she had been gone forever before she finally returned. "Okay Ms. Brown, we have your statement. I just need you to sign some things and you'll be free to go. If we need anything else from you, we'll contact you. If you need to speak to us in case there is something that you remember, here is my number." She handed Keisha a business card and waited a moment before saying anything else. "Ms. Brown, I know you were afraid for your life and your child's life, but we would've been able to help you a little better if you had said something when it first happened. If not for yourself, get some help for your son. It won't be good for him to see you so broken like this," the cop suggested.

Keisha didn't respond. She took the business card and tucked it in her sweatpants' pocket before leaving out of the interrogation room. Maurice stood up when he saw her. He gave her a hug and held her tight. Keisha was all cried out for the moment and was exhausted. They left the precinct and drove back to her house.

"Are you sure you want to stay here after what happened?" Jamal asked her.

Keisha looked around and took a deep breath. "They chased me from my first home. They're not going to chase me from this one." She headed up to her bedroom so she could straighten it up. They followed behind her.

"Keisha, what the hell happened? How did he get into the house?" Deisha asked as she helped Keisha clean up. Maurice told Keisha to have a seat and began straightening up with Deisha.

"Can somebody please open a fucking window? I can still smell Old Spice in here." Keisha asked as she sat on the dresser.

"My uncle installs home security systems. I'll have him come over and do the house for you before Manny and Kamir gets here," D-Ball said.

"Thank you," Keisha replied. "I don't know how he got in here. I locked all of the doors and windows. All I know is, I went to bed with my bedroom light on and when I woke up, the shit was off and I could smell Old Spice cologne. If I don't remember anything else about what happened in that damn holding cell, I remember the smell of his damn cologne. That shit stinks. As soon as I smelled it, I tried to get up and that's when he pinned me down." Keisha shook her head and stared off as if she could see what had happened to her on the wall. She shook her head again and continued. "When he started doing the stuff that he did to me in that holding cell, I just snapped. I bit his muthafucking hand like a muthafucking pit-bull and he hit me. Then I grabbed him and head butted his ass to get him off of me."

"Damn!" Maurice and Jamal said at the same time as they looked at Keisha.

"That's what the fuck I'm talking about," D-Ball said as he gave Keisha a pound.

"I started screaming for D-Ball and tried to get away but got tangled up in the sheets and fell off the bed. That's when he grabbed me by my hair and smacked me. I fell into the dresser. The lamp fell and when I heard him coming for me again, I grabbed the fucking lamp and tried to knock his lights out. Then I scrambled on the bed for my gun and I shot his ass."

The room was quiet for a moment. Deisha left and got a bucket of hot soapy water from the bathroom so she could try to scrub the blood stains from the carpet. Keisha tore the sheets from the bed and threw them in the trash before dressing the bed with fresh ones. They stayed with Keisha for an hour longer to make sure she was okay before they got ready to leave.

Maurice looked at her face. Though her eye wasn't swollen the way it was after the first attack, her cheek was puffy from the hits she took and she had two cuts on her lip. He shook his head in disgust.

"You never told Manny about the first time, did you?" he asked her. Keisha shook her head and looked at the floor. "So what are you going to do this time; come up with another lie?" Maurice asked.

"I don't know," she mumbled.

"You have to tell him. You cannot protect him from something like this, that's not your job. It's his job to protect you. Lying to him about getting raped and then lying to him about tonight not to mention you kept Ms. Becky's passing from him for almost a week, it's not a good look Keisha. You can't get through this by yourself."

"Maurice, you don't understand. I feel so dirty. I can't tell him."

"If you don't tell him, I will." Maurice said, firmly. "I'm not playing, Keisha." He hugged his little sister and kissed her cheek before leaving with Deisha.

Keisha heard D-Ball hammering something from the kitchen. She went inside to see what he was doing.

He had taken silver hooks from the kitchen drawers and was nailing them to the side panels of the back door. He then took a broom and laid it across the hooks to make sure no one could come through.

"Thank you," Keisha said.

"No problem. I'ma sleep on the couch. Let a muthafucka try to come through the front and I'ma pump 'em full of some hot shit." D-Ball said as he went back to the living room. Keisha followed behind him.

"Do you think Samir sent him again?" Keisha asked.

D-Ball thought for a moment. "Nah. Samir would've known that you wouldn't be here by yourself so he would've had someone with him to check to see who else was here and made sure my ass got smoked." D-Ball hesitated before speaking his next thought. "Sounds like the cop was just on some stalker shit and figured you were an easy target."

Keisha shuttered at the thought. She definitely didn't like the way that sounded. She looked at D-Ball as he placed a blanket on the sofa with a pillow. "Thank you," she said again.

"Stop thanking me, Keesh. You're like my little sister and you're Manny's girl. I'ma have y'all back no matter what. I just wish I could've done a better job at looking out for Kiree." He sat on the couch and put his hands to his face. He hadn't had a chance to mourn his friend either with everything that was going on. He struggled to keep his tears in, not wanting to cry in front of Keisha. She sat next to him and put her arm around him. She wasn't sure what to say to him. As long as she had known D-Ball, she had never seen him cry. It broke her heart knowing that he felt guilty for not being able to save Kiree. She wiped his eyes and told him that it would be okay. She kissed his forehead and rubbed the back of his neck. D-Ball looked at the bruises on her face and shook his head. He traced over her swollen cheek with his thumb and down to her lip. Before Keisha knew it, he kissed her. She froze for a moment but then kissed him back. The kiss went from being innocent to deep and passionate. D-Ball ran his fingers through her hair as he French kissed her deeply. But when his hands moved down to her neck, Keisha pulled away and jumped up. Flashes of the cop choking her came to mind. She lightly touched her neck where she had been choked and closed her eyes trying to push the memory from her mind.

"I'm sorry," D-Ball said.

Keisha shook her head but was unable to speak. She took a deep breath and then went to her room quietly as if nothing happened.

21

Maurice and Deisha made it back to her condo. She stood in her kitchen and shook her head at everything that had happened in the last week. Everything was unraveling and before they were given a chance to handle one tragedy, they were being hit with another. She was still trying to figure out a way to help her patient in the midst of her own personal drama while thinking of a way to get Keisha to agree to attend a support group for rape victims. She closed her eyes and rotated her neck before rubbing the back of it with her hand.

Maurice stood behind her and moved her hand so he could rub her neck for her. "What's wrong?" he asked her.

"Nothing, I'm just tired that's all," Deisha replied, enjoying the neck rub that he was giving her.

Maurice kissed her neck and hugged her from behind. "Come here," he said as he grabbed her by the hand and led her to the bathroom. Deisha had an enormous tub with golden brown ceramic tile covering her bathroom walls. Maurice had already ran a hot bubble bath and lit the scented candles that she had in there, placing them around the bath tub and on the shelves on her walls so that the bathroom held a golden glow. Deisha looked around at the way the flames' shadows danced on her walls. She smiled.

"You're always taking care of everybody else. Tonight, I just want to take care of you." Maurice said as he unbuttoned her blouse and began to undress her. Deisha surrendered to him and let him cater to her. He held her hand and helped her step into the hot water laced with a blanket of bubbles. Deisha closed her eyes as the water enveloped her body and immediately began to soothe her. She loved how large and deep her bath tub was. Maurice undressed and joined her. He positioned Deisha between his legs and took her loofa sponge and squeezed hot water onto her chest and down her arms. She leaned back on his chest and closed her eyes as he wrapped his arms around her and they relaxed.

Maurice played with her fingers as they talked. After nervously thinking over whether or not he should propose to Deisha for a second time, he reached behind one of the candles that he lit and pulled out a ring box. He took the ring out and slid it onto her finger. Deisha's eyes popped open and she looked at her hand with her mouth partially opened.

"Deisha, do you love me?" he whispered in her ear.

"Yes," she replied. She stared down at her hand as Maurice intertwined their fingers.

"I want to make you my wife before I make you a mother. Please don't tell me no, again."

"Maurice…" Deisha said. Her heart raced.

"You said you were scared that you couldn't keep me. I'm not going anywhere and like I said; you're already my wife, I just want it to be official. This last year without you was hell and I do not want us to go through that again. You're my best friend and my lover. I need you to be my wife," Maurice said to her.

Deisha squeezed his hand as her eyes became teary. Maurice waited nervously for her to say something and hoped that she was not about to turn him down for the second time. Her silence was beginning to unnerve him. He heard Deisha sniff and shifted in the tub so he could see her.

"Why are you crying?" he asked her.

Deisha opened her mouth to speak but couldn't form the words. Instead she nodded her head.

"Yeah?" Maurice asked making sure that's what she was saying.

"Yes," Deisha said as her voice cracked. "Yes, yes, yes, Maurice. Yes."

Maurice threw his fist in the air in victory and Deisha laughed. He kissed her longingly. "Those better be happy tears," he said to her.

Deisha laughed as he kissed her again. "Yes they are." She shifted back in the tub so she could lean on his chest. Butterflies filled her stomach as she thought of being Maurice's wife. She couldn't stop smiling and couldn't wait for her next Skype session with Chanda so she could share her good news.

When the water began to cool, Maurice got out of the tub and came back with towels for him and Deisha. He dried her off and then led her back to the bedroom, laying her on the bed. He rubbed lotion over her back, massaging her from her shoulders down to her calves. Deisha felt like she was in heaven. She turned over so she could face Maurice and traced her fingers over his chest and his abs. She stopped at the bullet wound that he had placed a fresh bandage over after getting out of the tub and touched it lightly. Maurice could tell what she was thinking; that she almost lost him.

"I'm not going anywhere," he said to her, hoping to ease her fears.

Deisha nodded as she continued to stare at the wound. Maurice grabbed her hand and kissed her palm. He then kissed her fingers before leaning close to her so he could kiss her. Deisha wrapped her arms and legs around him, kissing him back and inviting him in. They spent the remainder of the night together intimately for the first time in over a year.

22

Jamal had the pleasure of having a hotel suite to stay in while he worked with the Philadelphia Police Department at their expense. After taking a long shower and getting something to eat, he checked his cell phone and saw that he had several text messages and missed calls from his girlfriend Kareema. With everything that was going on, he hadn't been able to talk to her as much as he usually did and hadn't seen her since before he came to Philly more than a week prior. It was almost 2am and he knew she was more than likely asleep. He figured he would at least leave her a voice-mail.

"Hello," a sleepy voice answered.

Jamal wasn't expecting her to pick up. "Hey babe, I didn't mean to wake you. I was just going to leave you a message real quick and then hit you up tomorrow before I head to the candle light vigil."

"No, it's okay. I wanted to hear your voice. How is everything in Philly?" Kareema asked.

Jamal hadn't told her everything. As far as Kareema knew, Kiree was a cousin of his that had been murdered and he was temporarily assigned to the PPD to help with a major case. She had no idea that he was potentially in the middle of a drug war. "Yeah everything is as it can be expected. I just want to get this over with and come back home."

"I hate that I don't talk to you that much. Do you know when this will be over and you'll be back home?"

Jamal let out a deep sigh. "No, hopefully it won't be too long. But go ahead back to sleep. I just wanted to check in with you. I'll hit you up later."

"Okay babe. I love you," Kareema told him.

Jamal hesitated. "Ditto," he disconnected the call and sat his phone on the night stand.

He had been in a relationship with Kareema for almost two years. He was trying hard to open up to her but he hadn't been comfortable being in a relationship after what happened to Tamera. He knew Kareema was good for him and he tried hard not to compare her to Tammy. Sometimes he had doubts about their relationship. Though he cared deeply for her, he wasn't sure if he truly loved her.

Jamal turned out his light and turned the television on to ESPN. He didn't feel tired but as soon as he laid his head down, he fell asleep.

Jamal was walking down the street with a female. They were looking at pictures and laughing when a car pulled up and started shooting at them. Jamal tried desperately to pull his female companion to the ground but his hand slipped. He heard screams and tires screeching as a car sped off...

Jamal tossed in his sleep, changing his sleeping position...

Jamal burst through hospital doors. He looked around frantically. "Shawn! Tammy!" he called out as he looked around. He tried to push through a crowd of people when he thought he saw Tamera. Each time he tried pushing through she appeared to be further and further away. "TAMMY!" he called out.

"Jamal..." he heard a voice say from behind him. Jamal turned in the direction of that voice and saw Kareema in a white dress. The front was covered in blood...

Jamal jerked awake and sat straight up in his bed. "Kareema!" he said aloud as he clenched his sheets in his hand. He looked around his hotel room and then closed his eyes. His heart was racing and he was breathing heavy. *"Where the hell did that dream come from?"* he thought to himself. He rubbed his hands across his face and then looked at them. They were shaking. He balled his hands into fists and shook his head. He didn't like the feeling that the dream had left him with. Jamal prayed that nothing went wrong. He lay back down in the bed still shaken up from the dream. Sleep was not going to come easy to him again.

. . .

Jamal was finishing up his breakfast the next morning when he heard a knock at his hotel room's door. He grabbed his gun from off of the night stand and made his way over to his door taking a quick peek out of the peep hole. When he saw Davidson, he let out a nervous sigh and put the safety on his gun.

"I thought I told you to call me before you came through here?" Jamal said as he opened the door for Davidson and let him in.

"I did call. I called a couple times but it just rang and went straight to voice-mail. So I just came on over to make sure everything was cool," Davidson explained as he came in and sat down.

Jamal looked at his phone and saw that the ringer was off. He shook his head. "My bad, it's been a long night."

"What's going on?" Davidson asked.

"The punk cop who raped Keisha in her holding cell had been following her around and attacked her at her house last night. She ended up shooting him."

Davidson looked at Jamal with wide eyes. "You've gotta be fucking kidding me! Samir sent him?"

"I thought that at first, but nah. He wouldn't have just sent the cop by himself. He would've done a surveillance to see if any of us would be there so he could send an ambush that would be more effective than the ones he sent before. I think the cop was just stalking her figuring she was an easy target," Jamal explained as he poured himself a glass of orange juice.

Davidson shook his head. "That girl has been through hell and back this past week."

"Shit, she can't even make it back, shit just keeps happening," Jamal replied.

"So where is she now?"

"She's back at her house. Maurice and Deisha helped her clean up and D-Ball is having someone come over to install an alarm system."

"This shit is crazy," Davidson replied. He reached in his bag and pulled a folder out. "I have something that you might want to look at."

"What is that?" Jamal asked as he drank his orange juice. Davidson just nodded at it. Jamal sat his cup down and opened the folder. He looked at the contents confused but then his facial expression changed completely. He stared at a picture of a man and it was almost like looking at an older version of himself. He was looking at his father's file. "Where did you get this?" Jamal asked.

"Read it," Davidson suggested. Jamal looked at Davidson for a space of heartbeats and then began pacing with the folder in his hand as he read it. His eyes widened and then he looked at Davidson.

"You've gotta be fucking kidding me," Jamal replied.

"I couldn't make anything up like this. Your father was an informant for the 22nd District. They were well aware a long time ago of dirty cops on the force. They never suspected Kristoff; they suspected his partner Smitty, the guy your father was working for. His name was Christian Smith AKA Smitty. Smitty wanted out. Now I'm guessing that Kristoff flipped evidence on Smitty to have him arrested and learned that your father was an informant for the cops. Maybe your father knew Smitty was going to drop the dime on Kristoff and Samir and whoever else was working for them back then. And I believe that is why Samir killed your father."

Jamal stood in front of Davidson unable to speak. The anger was so heavy within him that he could hear a ringing in his ears.

"This is a lot deeper than you expected; deeper than I expected."

Jamal shook his head. "So what now? What difference does this make now? My father is dead, Smitty is dead, Kristoff is dead. Samir is the only motherfucker still standing and we still don't know who is backing him on the inside."

"I showed it to you to give you closure, to let you know what was really going on." Davidson replied.

"But it doesn't fucking matter now. All that matters is taking Samir out before he does anything else." Jamal argued.

"Take him out?" Davidson asked. "Jamal, I never said I wanted you to kill him. We're doing this by the book."

Jamal looked at Davidson as if he were crazy. "By the book? Are you fucking serious? Nigga, the book has his back! How the fuck are we supposed to go up against something like that? They're killing cops to cover their asses. They're killing their own! And you think we'll be able to take him down through the legal system when you see for yourself how corrupt the justice system is?!"

"We're not all that way, Jamal. I'm not and you're not and I'm positive the good outweighs the bad. We have a duty to our badge…"

"Fuck that," Jamal cut him off. "I have a duty to my life, to my family; to the friends I have left that haven't been killed by his bitch-ass. You can't take him down through the legal system because as you said yourself, this shit is bigger than Samir."

Davidson waited a moment before speaking. "Maybe it's because we come from two different backgrounds, but I trust that he can be stopped through the proper legal channels. And I need for you to trust that, too. That's the only way this team is going to work."

Jamal shook his head in disagreement. He thought that Davidson was naïve and blind to everything that was going on. Samir was not going to be stopped through the legal system and if Davidson didn't understand that soon, he was going to get himself as well as Jamal killed.

"Listen, I'll make a deal with you. If we can't get him legally, then we do things your way." Davidson said.

"You're problem is, you're still trying to play by the rules and abide by the law and uphold your badge while going up against people who fight dirty and flat out don't give a fuck. I'ma do what I gotta do. I'm not about to fuck around and get killed on some Action Jackson shit." Jamal tossed the folder that contained his father's information onto the table before leaving the room.

ATR 2: Jamal's Return

23

Keisha awoke the next morning. She stayed in bed for a little while thinking over the things that had happened during the last week. She specifically thought about what happened the night before with D-Ball and their kiss. She felt guilty and was partially afraid to come out of the room and face him. Keisha told herself that they didn't have sex and it was just an innocent kiss in the heat of a moment brought on by constant drama from the last week. She took a deep breath and decided to just face what happened. She grabbed a change of clothes and a towel and headed to her bathroom so she could get showered and dressed and pick up Manny and Kamir. Thankfully, D-Ball was not upstairs. After getting dressed, she went downstairs and saw D-Ball eating a bowl of cereal.

"Hey," she said as she went over to a mirror to put on her make-up.

"Yo," D-Ball said without looking up from his bowl of cereal.

Keisha looked at herself closely in the mirror as she was about to apply foundation to her face. She thought about what Maurice said the night before and stopped. There was no point in trying to hide the bruises. Manny needed to know what happened. She shook her head and tossed her make-up back into her hand bag.

"Are you coming with me to get Manny?" Keisha asked D-Ball as she put her coat on.

D-Ball got up to get his coat but wouldn't look at her. "Yeah, you want me to take you or just follow you in my car?"

"Can you take me? When Manny sees my face, he's gonna fucking flip and I'ma have to tell him everything. He's going to be pissed because I didn't tell him when it first happened so I just want somebody there that will keep him calm." Keisha explained.

"No problem," D-Ball said.

They got inside of the car and drove over to the hospital in silence. D-Ball suggested she stay in the car to avoid Manny snapping in the hospital again. Keisha smiled when she saw Manny coming over to the car with D-Ball. As he was getting into the back with her, she leaned over to pretend she was fixing her shoes. She waited until he sat next to her before she sat up. He was about to give her a hug and a kiss when he noticed the bruises on her cheek and on her lip.

"What happened to your face, Keisha?" Manny asked her as he looked her over.

"Promise you won't get mad," Keisha said.

"Depends on what you're about to tell me." Manny replied.

"Manny, please. I need you to understand that I didn't tell you right away because of everything that was going on and the doctors said the less stress on you the better your chances were of healing without complications."

"Keisha, what the fuck happened?" Manny asked again.

Keisha took a deep breath and told Manny everything that happened from the ambush at their apartment which led to her killing a man along with what happened to her in the holding cell and at the house the night before. Just as she thought, Manny snapped.

"Why the fuck didn't you tell me when it first happened?!" Manny seethed. "What the fuck, Keisha?! You sitting here lying in my face about so much shit. You lied about my mom, you lied about this! I'm your fucking man; you don't keep shit like this from me! I don't give a fuck what the doctors suggested. This ain't their fucking relationship. They ain't the ones that gotta get through this, it's us!" Manny was hot.

Keisha put her hands to her face and cried. "You think it was easy for me to keep this from you!? You're mad I didn't tell you, I get that! But did you even think that maybe it's hard for me to tell what they fucking did to me! It's hard for me to talk about it! I don't want to fucking talk about it because when I talk about it, I see it, I feel it, I hear his voice, I smell his cologne! It's like it's happening all over again!" Keisha didn't mean to yell but she was angry and hurting just as much as Manny was. D-Ball stayed outside of the car to let them have their moment. Manny put his arms around Keisha and held her.

"I'm sorry, babe. I didn't mean to go off. I can't fucking believe that nigga sent his goons after you and my fucking son and then had some punk-ass pig do you like that. I should've walked away when you asked me to and none of this would've happened," Manny said as he held Keisha.

"It's too late to worry about that now. Let's just focus on the candle light vigil for Kiree and your mom. Let's get Kamir because I know he misses his daddy. And I missed you too," Keisha said as she pulled away from him and wiped her face.

Manny looked at Keisha as he held her face. He was still pissed but kept his cool. He knew Keisha had held things down for him while he was in the hospital and he knew she was trying to keep it together with everything that happened to her not to mention the fact that she shot two men and killed one. Keisha had taken care of him while he was down and now it was time for him to take care of her.

D-Ball drove them over to Keisha's mother's house. Manny looked at Keisha's face again and shook his head.

"You're mom doesn't know, does she?" Manny asked her. Keisha looked away and shook her head. He let out an angry sigh. "Babe, you can't keep lying about this. Especially to your mom."

"Manny, I can't tell her yet. I will after everything calms down and starts going back to normal. But right now," Keisha shook her head. "I need to deal with us and our son and get through this funeral Monday."

Manny stared at her for a moment and then kissed her briefly. "I'll come in with you."

They got out of D-Ball's car and walked onto Ms. Brown's porch holding each other's hand. Keisha took out her keys and unlocked the door. She knew her mother was home because she saw her car out front. Kamir was sitting in the living room watching the old Jim Henson's *Teenage Mutant Ninja Turtles* movie and eating cheesy crackers. When he saw his mother and father, he jumped up and ran to them. Keisha picked him up and they both hugged and kissed him.

"Mommy, Daddy!" Kamir said with glee. He wrapped his tiny arms around his father's neck.

"What's up, Lil' Man? What does your G-mom have you in here watching?" Manny asked his son as he held him.

"Turtles," Kamir said with a grin.

"Aw snap! This was the bomb movie when I was a kid," Manny said as he sat on the couch with his son. Keisha smiled down at them.

"Keisha? I didn't even hear you come in," Ms. Brown said from the kitchen. It smelled like she was frying chicken. "Come on in here. How are you, Manny?"

"I'm fine, Ms. Charlene." Manny replied from the living room.

Keisha took a deep breath and made her way into the kitchen. "Hey, mom."

"Hey baby," Ms. Brown said before looking at her. She turned to give her a hug but stopped dead in her tracks. She looked Keisha's face over and leaned back. She then threw her hands to her face. "Oh no, Keisha. What the hell happened to your face this time?

And don't stand here and tell me another bold faced lie about a fight you got into!" Ms. Brown fumed.

"Mom, I'm alright," Keisha replied, avoiding the question.

"I didn't ask you that shit," Ms. Brown said angrily. "What the hell is going on? Are you in some kind of trouble?"

"No mom," Keisha replied quickly.

"Keisha, got damn it, this is the second time your face has looked like someone tried to use you as a punching bag. Now I know it wasn't Manny, thank God, because he was in the hospital. But something is going on and you need to tell me what it is."

Keisha took a deep breath trying to keep her composure. "Mom, it's just been a lot going on and I really can't get into it right now. But when things calm down, we'll talk. I promise."

"That's not good enough, Keisha." Ms. Brown said as she shook her head at her.

"Well mom, it's going to have to be good enough. I can't do this right now. I need to help Manny get his strength back, I need to make sure that the candle light vigil and memorial service for Kiree and Ms. Becky are taken care of, and I need to take care of my son."

Ms. Brown interrupted her. "And while you're taking care of everything and everybody, who is taking care of you?" She placed her hands on Keisha's face and frowned at her bruises. "He's the reason all of this is going on. When are you going to wise up...?"

Keisha snatched away from her mother and looked at her with contempt. "Don't do this now, mom. Don't pass judgment. I love Manny and he loves me. He's a good father to my son, he's a good man to me and provides and protects us like a man should. So what he doesn't have the corporate job, or isn't a teacher or doctor or lawyer or engineer! So what! He's a helluva lot more responsible than some of these shirt and tie wearing fakes outside these doors! He loves me and Kamir, mom. He respects me and treats me well. Let that be enough."

"He loves you? He respects you? How is he protecting you when men are gunning after you, your brother and your son because of choices that he's made?! The life he chose to live is becoming detrimental to both you and your son. I do not want to have to bury my child!" Ms. Brown said in tears.

Keisha turned her back on her mother and leaned onto the kitchen counter. She took multiple deep breaths to keep from crying before she turned back to her mother and hugged her. "You won't be burying me anytime soon, mom. I promise." She kissed her mother on the cheek before letting her go. "Is that for the memorial service?" she asked as she pointed to the chicken that her mother was frying.

Ms. Brown wiped her face and then washed her hands. "Yeah, I made some potato salad, baked macaroni and cheese and some cabbage to take to Becky's house. Do you want me to call you later when it's done so you can come back to get it and take it back to her house?"

"You're not coming?" Keisha asked with her eye brows raised.

"No. I'll be at the funeral Monday but I'm not coming to the vigil."

Keisha nodded. "Okay. Well, we're going to leave. We have a few things to take care of before tonight. Thanks for making the food, mom. I'll be back to pick everything up and we'll talk soon. I promise." Ms. Brown walked Keisha to the living room.

"I'll hold you to that promise. Come here, Kamir."

Kamir jumped from the couch and ran over to Ms. Brown. She picked him up and hugged him. "You be good, you hear me? And later this week we'll bake a sock-it-to-me cake like I promised, okay?"

"Okay, G-Mom." Kamir said with a smile. She put him down and helped him put his coat and hat on.

"Good seeing you, Manny." Ms. Brown said, forcing a smile.

"You too, Ms. Charlene." Manny stood up and took Kamir's hand. They left the house and went to D-Ball's car. They went back to the house in Glenolden to wait for D-Ball's uncle to install the alarm system. Once they were finished, they went to Ms. Becky's house to get ready for the candle light vigil that was to start at 7pm. Family and friends from all over were in town for the funeral Monday. They greeted Keisha, Manny and their son with hugs and kisses when they arrived at the house. Most of the afternoon and early evening was spent reminiscing as tears of sorrow and laughter were shared.

Manny heard what Ms. Brown said to Keisha in the kitchen and was glad that Keisha stood up to her the way that she did. But he knew her mother was right; they wouldn't be in the mess they were in now if he hadn't been in the streets. He rationalized many times that he wanted to make sure he could provide for his family without having to struggle and that he also wanted to make sure that Keisha was able to get her degree. But at the end of the day, he knew he had made more than enough money and could have gotten out a long time ago. He couldn't change the past, it was over and done. But he promised to make things right for their future and insure that this situation did not happen again.

Manny went up to his mother's room while his aunts, uncles and cousins were downstairs talking. He looked around and imagined what she had been doing before she received the devastating news that her oldest son had been murdered and her younger son was critically wounded as well. He noticed the ironing board was up and sheets and towels were folded on her bed. Judging by the curtains that lay across her dresser, he was betting that she was about to put them up. He walked over to her closet and touched the long leather coat that he bought for her a couple of years before. He put his face to it and smelled it. He could smell his mother in the material; the cucumber and melon body spray that she loved to wear and a hint of Shea butter she always wore to keep her skin smooth. His heart ached for his mother and his brother.

"Mom…" Manny said, becoming choked up. He took the coat from the closet and sat on the side of her bed, holding it up to his face. "Mom," he said again.

Keisha stood in the doorway watching him, feeling his pain. She sat next to him and put her arm around him. Manny cried his heart out for his mother and for his brother.

Noticing that his mommy and daddy weren't in the living room with the rest of the family, Kamir came upstairs to Ms. Becky's bedroom. He stood in front of his father and tried to move the coat so he could see his face.

"Why come you're crying, Daddy?" Kamir asked in a tiny voice.

Normally, Keisha would correct his speech but she decided to let it go for the moment. "Daddy is sad right now, honey."

"Because G-Mom and Uncle Kiree went to heaven?" Kamir asked as he looked at his mother.

Keisha forced a smile and nodded her head as she tried to fight back the tears. "Yes baby, G-Mom and Kiree are in heaven now."

"When are they coming back?" Kamir asked.

Keisha looked up at the ceiling and let out a deep sigh. She wiped the tears that pricked the corners of her eyes and then looked back at her son. "They're not Kay-baby. But they'll always be with us and they'll always watch over us and protect us. The way to keep them with you is to remember them. Keep them here," Keisha said as she pointed to Kamir's head, "and in here," she said, pointing to his heart. Kamir nodded his head.

Yani

Manny had calmed down a bit and wiped his face.
He hugged his son tightly with one arm and pulled
Keisha close to him with the other arm. He kissed her
and shook his head. "I love you, Keesh. Thank you for
staying with me. Thank you for giving me my son and
thank you for holding it down and protecting him
when I couldn't," he said in a low voice.

"I love you, too. And don't thank me. I played my
part as I should and I would do it again in a heartbeat,"
Keisha told him. They stayed in his mother's room for
a little while longer until his aunt called for them so
they could head over to 24th and Oxford Streets for the
candle light service. Keisha sent Kamir downstairs just
as D-Ball was coming up. He handed a gun to Keisha.

"What's this for?" Manny asked.

"I'm not taking any chances," Keisha replied as
she pulled the clip from the gun to make sure it was
loaded and then slammed it back in. She put the safety
on and tucked it in the small of her back, pulling her
shirt and jacket down over it to keep it concealed.

"Wait a fucking minute. Keisha, your job is not to
protect me. That's my job," Manny said as he stared at
her.

"Manny, I love you but don't debate me." Keisha
said as she stared back at him.

Manny shook his head. "Do not treat me like getting shot crippled me. I'm not handicapped."

"I'm not saying that. But you just got out of the hospital. You could have died! We're about to bury Kiree and your mom. I don't want to bury you, too!" Keisha hissed.

Manny nodded his head. "I'ma let this go for now. We'll talk when we get home."

D-Ball checked the clips to both of his guns and put them in the small of his back. They went downstairs where more people had gathered. A crowd was outside waiting for the queue to leave. The plan was to march from Ms. Becky's house on 27th and Jefferson Street over to 24th and Oxford. Keisha marveled at the many people who came out to show support. She spotted Jamal, Deisha and Maurice and gave them each a hug. They passed out candles to everyone. Some people showed up in hoodies that had Kiree's likeness on the front and back. Others had Ms. Becky's photo and some had both.

"Thanks everybody for coming out. This means a lot to me and the Stephens family. Ms. Becky's death and Kiree's murder were a devastating and preventable loss. The purpose of tonight is for us to come together peacefully and determined to let these thugs know we're tired of turning the other cheek while they destroy our neighborhoods, kill our men, rape our women and leave our children fatherless and unprotected. It's a vicious cycle that needs to stop! We can't expect political figures to come in and correct our shit if we're not willing to correct it ourselves. It starts with us first!" Keisha said loudly. Shouts of agreement and clapping could be heard among the crowd. "I'm going to light the first candle and then what we're going to do is pass the flame in honor of Kiree and Ms. Becky's name. And then we're walking to the spot where Kiree was murdered. Please, no fighting. That's what they expect us to do whenever Black people turn out in numbers like this. Let's show them we're more than what they portray us to be on TV! We love you Kiree and Ms. Becky! Rest in Peace!!" More cheers were heard from the crowd as others shouted "Rest in Peace Kiree." Keisha lit the first candle and passed the flame to Manny who passed it to D-Ball and the flame went around from there until golden glows lit up the dark night in front of Ms. Becky's house.

A young woman in the crowd began singing "Precious Lord" loudly as the march began. Others joined in and sang along as they marched over to 24th and Oxford Streets. Keisha held Manny's hand and D-Ball placed Kamir on his shoulders. Maurice held

Keisha's other hand and Deisha held his and Jamal's hands. When they arrived at the corner where Kiree had been murdered, Keisha and Manny looked at the memorial the neighborhood left. Teddy bears, candles, signs with short poems and messages of condolences covered the side walk. Jamal made sure there was a police presence at the candle light vigil just in case Samir had any ideas. D-Ball stood near Keisha and Manny with one hand in the small of his back just in case he had to draw his gun.

The candle light vigil was started with Keisha leading the Lord's Prayer. She and Manny shared a few words with Manny doing his best not to share his grief for his loss in front of the crowd. After others shared brief memories of Kiree and expressed their condolences, they had a moment of silence before placing the candles along with the other memorial items on the ground. Keisha hugged Manny tightly before the crowd broke up and they made their way back to Ms. Becky's house. Deisha's aunt cooked food for her to bring to the house as well and the family and close friends sat down to eat and drink, sharing more laughs and memories. Deisha followed Keisha into the kitchen.

"How are you holding up?" Deisha asked her.

"Pretty good," Keisha replied as she washed dishes.

"Your speech was amazing and on point. I'm so proud of how strong you've been throughout all of this. But Keisha, you've got to slow down. You need time to grieve, too." Deisha suggested.

Keisha sighed, "Deisha, only one of us can break down at a time. I need to stay busy because if I'm still for too long it gives me a chance to think, to feel and to remember shit that happened. And I don't want to right now. I'm fine though. I really am." Keisha rinsed the dishes and dried them before putting them away. She then began packing up plates of food for people to take with them. Deisha understood where Keisha was coming from. She remembered how she shut down when Tamera was killed and did everything possible to keep busy so she didn't have to let it sink in that her best friend was gone. It wasn't until Deisha heard a voicemail that Tamera left her days before she was murdered that she broke down. She remembered Maurice coming to her dorm room to console her and she looked down at the ring on her finger.

"Keisha, guess what?" Deisha asked with a smile on her face.

"What's up?" Keisha asked as she put the food inside of the refrigerator.

Deisha held up her left hand with a huge grin on her face. Keisha did a double take and then her mouth hung open.

"Maurice asked you again?!" Keisha squealed. Deisha nodded. "And you said yes?!" she squealed again as she grabbed her hand so she could get a closer look.

"Yes!!!" Deisha replied. They jumped up and down.

"Oh my God! I know I'm a bridesmaid." Keisha gushed as she marveled over the ring on Deisha's finger.

"Of course. Chanda will be my maid of honor and you will be a bridesmaid." Deisha said.

"I'm so happy for you guys. I knew y'all would get back together."

Deisha smiled. "I was hoping so. I messed up but I'm so grateful your brother was able to forgive me."

"So how did he ask; did he get down on one knee; hide the ring in a cupcake?" They giggled together.

"No, and I'm glad because that's so corny and cliché." They laughed some more. "He ran me a hot bubble bath after we came back from your place last night. While we were in the tub, he slid the ring on my finger and told me that I was already his wife; he just wanted to make it official. He said I was his best friend and his lover and he needed me to be his wife. There was no way I was going to tell him no again."

"Aww," Keisha gushed. "That is great. With all of this madness going on, we need something wonderful. And how do Black people celebrate something wonderful?" Keisha peeped in the dining room to make sure no one was looking and pulled a bottle of Moscato from the cabinet. "We drink!"

Deisha burst out laughing. "No you didn't hide a bottle in here."

"Shiiiid, hell yeah! Let them niggas drink the corny shit." They laughed as Keisha pulled out a few wine glasses. She called Manny, D-Ball, Jamal and Maurice into the kitchen.

"What's up?" Jamal asked as they came into the kitchen.

Keisha poured them all a drink and passed them each a glass. "Raise your cups for my brother and the only woman for him. I want to congratulate them on their engagement." Keisha said with a huge grin.

Jamal looked at Maurice and Deisha wide eyed. "Whaaaaat!!!" he slapped Maurice a handshake and then looked at Deisha's hand. "Damn girl, you're gonna have to do finger curls to hold that shit up!" Deisha laughed as Jamal hugged her.

"Congrats," Manny said as he tapped his glass against Deisha's and Maurice's glasses. They all took a drink and then Keisha poured them a little more.

"Ay yoo! I can't be getting drunk now. I just got home." Manny joked. They laughed together as Keisha sat the bottle down.

"Boy, hush," Keisha giggled. "Raise your cups one more time for Kiree and Ms. Becky. May God keep them safe and wrapped in his unconditional love. And may he keep us and protect us from our enemies…"

Maurice interrupted her. "Without us losing anymore friends."

"Amen," Manny said as he raised his drink. They tapped their glasses together and drank.

"Manny, we need to talk to you." Jamal said as he placed his glass in the sink. He looked at Keisha and Deisha to let them know what the conversation was going to be about.

"Come in the living room with me Deisha, so these people don't realize we got the better drinks in here and bum-rush us."

Deisha laughed and followed Keisha into the living room knowing what Jamal wanted to talk about with Manny.

"What's up, yo?" Manny asked Jamal.

"We need your help with something," Jamal said.

"Something like what?"

Jamal explained to Manny why he was still in Philly and what Detective Davidson wanted him to do. Though Davidson's plan was to take Samir down by the book; their plans were to take him out Street Justice style.

"So what, are y'all trying to ban together to take Samir out?" Manny asked.

"Fucking right," D-Ball replied.

Manny looked at Maurice. "You in on this, too?"

"He came after me and my sister. His ass gotta go," Maurice said with a straight face. "Not to mention what he had that punk-ass cop do to her in that holding cell and what could've happened to Kamir."

Manny thought of his brother and how he tried to warn Kiree that something bad was about to happen. He thought of what could've happened to his son and Keisha had he and D-Ball not trained her to use a gun. He shook his head as fury began to rise in him. "I'm in."

"My man," D-Ball said as he slapped Manny a handshake. Jamal shook his hand, too.

"Alright, we're going to meet at my hotel room Tuesday to work out some details. Everybody's gotta be on point because we're only gonna get one shot at this shit. If anything goes wrong, if anybody freezes up, it can get us all killed. Now I'm not gonna lie to y'all. We might get hurt or worse. So if you want to back out, I won't stop you." Jamal looked at everyone in the room. Nobody backed down.

"What about you, 'Mal? You're about to go up against your own cousin. You don't feel conflicted or anything?" Manny asked.

"Not at all," Jamal replied honestly. He thought about what D-Ball said to him and started to think that he was right. If he had the courage to take Samir down years ago, this probably wouldn't be happening, lives would not have been lost or destroyed. It was no point in wondering about the "what ifs". Things were happening now and Samir needed to be stopped now. Jamal just prayed that he didn't lose anyone else to the madness.

24

After returning to their new home in Glenolden, Keisha and Manny gave their son a bath and then played the Wii with him for a little while before putting him to bed. Keisha stood in the doorway and watched Manny as he read *Stone Soup* to Kamir until he fell asleep. Manny put the book away but continued to watch his son sleeping. Keisha walked behind Manny and put her arms around his waist.

Manny grabbed her hand and kissed it.

"Are you okay?" Keisha asked him.

"I'm alright, I guess. But I'm not ready for Monday. I'm not ready to bury my brother and my mom." Manny replied.

"I know babe, but I'll be with you. You won't be going through this alone."

Manny turned around and hugged Keisha tightly. He was so grateful to have her in his life. He didn't know what he would do or where he would be without her and their son. They retreated to their bedroom and lay down to watch a movie together before falling asleep.

Deisha got on Skype with Chanda to share her good news. Chanda was extremely excited for Deisha and happy that she and Maurice were finally able to swallow their prides and get back together. They secretly joked about having a double wedding together. Chanda was sad that they wouldn't be home for Thanksgiving in light of the drama that was going on in Philly. She promised Deisha if everything was calm by Christmas, they would be home around that time so they could hang out and wedding shop together.

Jamal had been keeping an eye on the warehouse Samir had taken him to and noticed that it seemed to be the meeting place for Samir when he did his business. Samir always took the same three guys with him which were the ones that were with him the day he made Jamal take the ride with him. That made it an even playing field for Jamal since he was going to have Manny, Maurice and D-Ball with him. He made a note that there were two entry points; one in the front and one in the back. He used that information to map out a plan to take out Samir.

Knowing that he was a target, Jamal began wearing his bullet proof vest at the suggestion of D-Ball. D-Ball too wore a bullet proof vest. Jamal made sure he ordered a vest for Manny and Maurice as well as Keisha. He had a sneaky suspicion that Keisha was going to need it. He noticed that she kept her gun with her the night of the candle light vigil. Jamal never would've guessed that Keisha would be the type to shoot first and ask questions later; Mentality of a rider.

The morning of Kiree and Ms. Becky's funeral arrived quickly. Keisha, Manny and their son got ready early with D-Ball. She grabbed her gun and was about to put it in the small of her back again, but Manny stopped her.

"Keesh, we're going to be in a church and a graveyard. I don't think anything is going to pop off today. Leave that home," Manny told her.

Keisha hesitated having a feeling deep in her gut that she should take the gun with her. But she didn't want Manny to think that she did not trust his judgment. She removed the clip from the gun, put it in its lockbox and sat it in the top of their closet out of their son's reach. They climbed into Keisha's car and drove to Ms. Becky's house with D-Ball following behind.

The family limo arrived shortly after Manny and Keisha were in the house greeting other family members. Jamal, Maurice and Deisha showed up and they waited until it was time to get to the funeral.

Deisha, Maurice and Jamal stayed with Keisha, Manny and their family so they could walk in together. Manny held it together until he reached Kiree's casket. Looking at his older brother set him off and he lost it. Keisha did her best to hold him up but he was almost on the floor with his legs giving way. Jamal tried to help her hold him up to get him to his seat. His grief and loud sobs were upsetting their son and he began to cry as well. They sat in the second row with Keisha cradling him in her arms as they cried together. Deisha, Maurice, Jamal and D-Ball sat behind them. Jamal and D-Ball were busy looking at the obituaries but Deisha was watching the people who came in to view Kiree and Ms. Becky. She noticed a tall man who had a stocky build walk over to Kiree's casket. He was light-skinned, possibly Puerto-Rican, and dressed in an all in one gray Dickie suit with a pair of Timberland boots. He stared at Kiree for a moment expressionless and then looked at Keisha and Manny. Deisha stared at him, waiting to see if he was going to view Ms. Becky as well. But when she saw the way he looked at Manny, she caught a bad feeling. D-Ball bent over to tie his shoe, not paying attention to anything and was unseen to the man in the Dickie suit. But the visitor noticed Jamal and turned to leave as quickly as he arrived.

Yani

"Did you just see that shit?" Deisha asked Maurice, disregarding the fact that she was using profanity in a church.

"Yeah, I saw that shit," Maurice said in a low voice as he looked behind him. He didn't see if the guy sat down or left so he faced forward. He too had a bad feeling.

"Am I crazy or did it look like he was checking to make sure Kiree was dead?" Deisha asked.

"That's exactly what it looked like. Aww man. This shit got me feeling sick. I got a bad feeling," Maurice replied.

"A bad feeling like what, what are y'all talking about?" Jamal asked.

Deisha whispered to him what she and Maurice had noticed with the last guy who came in to view Kiree and the way he looked at Manny.

"Shiiiiid," Jamal mumbled as he looked around. "I didn't think to have the cops outside of the church." He pulled out his phone and texted Detective Davidson asking him to come to the church where the funeral was being held and to have a unit on stand-by just in case.

"Jamal, are you carrying?" Maurice asked.

"Fucking right I'm carrying. Shit, I'm in Philly. I don't go no-where without my burner." Jamal replied.

He elbowed D-Ball. "Yo dawg, I know you're carrying."

"When am I never carrying?" D-Ball replied. "Why what's going on?"

Jamal leaned over and whispered in D-Ball's ear, telling him what Deisha had just said. D-Ball looked around and then turned sideways so the people sitting next to him couldn't see him pull his gun out. He checked the clip to make sure it was fully loaded and then eased it back where he took it from. He then checked his other one.

"I don't believe this shit," D-Ball said as he shook his head. His palms were sweating as the funeral proceeded. Jamal, Maurice, Deisha and D-Ball were all nervous but did not want to alarm Manny or Keisha. Jamal checked his phone and saw Davidson texted him back letting him know a unit would be on the corner and he was in the back of the church. Jamal turned around and looked. Davidson nodded at him.

Jamal turned back around and whispered to D-Ball. "Keep Keisha, Manny and Kamir behind you when we leave. I'ma stay on your right and Davidson will be on your left, cool?"

"Got you," D-Ball replied. They waited out the funeral and finally, the recessional was under way. Little by little, the packed church moved past the two caskets to say their farewells. D-Ball leaned next to Keisha as they stood to the side. "When we walk out of here; you, Kamir and Manny stay behind me and Jamal." He grabbed her hand and made her touch the small of his back where his gun was. "Pull my gun when you need it." D-Ball said to her in a low voice. Keisha looked at him puzzled but then nodded her head. The Pall Bearers grabbed the caskets and began walking out of the church. Keisha's heart was pounding in her chest. She stayed close behind D-Ball with Manny and her son at her side. Jamal walked ahead of them but close to D-Ball with Deisha and Maurice behind him. As they were walking down the stairs, Deisha looked around. She searched the crowd wildly for the man she saw in the church. By the time she saw him, it was too late.

"That's him," Deisha said to Jamal as she jerked on his arm. Another gunman came from the left and pulled his gun. Keisha pushed Manny and her son back with her left hand as she pulled the gun from D-Ball's back with her right. D-Ball pulled his other gun and fired at the man in the all in one Dickie suit as Keisha fired at the one coming towards them. People screamed and started running, pushing to get out of the way. Jamal took two shots to his torso and fell back. D-Ball turned and fired at the other gunman as Davidson fired at him also. Manny grabbed his son and ran back inside of the church. The scene outside of the church was chaotic as people either fell or was knocked down while others pushed and shoved to keep from getting shot. More cops came and grabbed D-Ball and Keisha. Davidson ran over to Jamal to check him. He was almost in a panic hoping that nothing bad happened to Jamal. When he felt the bullet proof vest, he let out a sigh of relief. Jamal was disoriented as he tried opening the vest. It felt like there was too much pressure against his chest. He coughed as he took deep breaths.

"DEISHA!" Maurice called out.

Jamal looked over in their direction and scrambled towards them. Deisha lay on the steps unconscious but still breathing. A bullet hit her in her stomach. Jamal grabbed Maurice and pulled him back.

"I've gotta stay with her, man! I've gotta stay with her!" Maurice screamed as he struggled against Jamal.

"Listen to me! Listen to me, Maurice! Let the medics do their jobs. She's going to be alright. Your sister and her son need you." Jamal said firmly to Maurice. Maurice was trembling as he turned to look at Deisha. The medics were placing her on a stretcher and putting her in the back of an ambulance.

"I've been where you are, Mar. But you've gotta keep a clear head for Deisha, for yourself and for your sister and her son."

Manny walked out of the church carrying his son in his arms. It took him a moment to calm Kamir down. Davidson was able to talk the police out of arresting Keisha and D-Ball since they both had a license to carry and his guns were registered. Keisha grabbed her son and felt all over his back, checking him to make sure he was okay.

"He's good, I checked him." Manny told her. Keisha fell into his arms and cried hysterically. "They shot Deisha!!" She sobbed in his arms.

Manny held Keisha and looked over at D-Ball with his son. He looked at Jamal and Maurice and saw how distraught he was that Deisha had been shot. He was beyond pissed off and tired.

"Jamal," Manny called over to him.

Jamal walked over to him and Keisha. "Yo."

"Samir didn't even have the fucking courtesy to let me bury my muthafucking mom and brother. He brought the bullshit to their funeral. To their funeral!! You tell that fucking cop he can either bring Samir in tonight or fish his fucking body outta Cobbs Creek tomorrow. He ain't playing by any rules, why the fuck should we!?" Manny said furiously.

Jamal looked at Manny and Keisha but didn't have the words to say. He knew Manny was right. He went back over to the cops to assist with the investigation and answer any necessary questions. When they were given the go ahead, Manny and his family headed over to Chelten Hills Cemetery to bury Kiree and Ms. Becky. Jamal and Maurice stayed behind so they could head over to the hospital to check on Deisha.

Maurice sat in a chair in the waiting room leaning on his knees with his hands to his head, shaking his leg. Jamal felt bad for him. He prayed that Deisha made it. He didn't want Maurice to go through the same thing that he went through with Tamera.

They waited a little longer when a doctor finally came over to them. Maurice stood up. His heart was racing in his chest as he waited to hear what the doctor had to say.

"Ms. Burton was stabilized. It was touch and go for a moment, we almost lost her. The bullet is lodged in some muscular tissue and she had some internal bleeding. We were able to get that under control. She'll be taken into surgery in the next ten minutes. Thankfully the bullet hasn't traveled. Once we remove it and repair any damage, she should make a full recovery," the doctor explained.

Maurice nodded his head and sat back down.

Jamal sat next to him when the doctor left. "She's going to be okay," Jamal told Maurice.

"You don't know that," Maurice said as he shook his head.

"No, I don't know that. But I believe that she will be okay. And you need to, too. You have to stay positive for her. Trust me on this," Jamal said to his friend. Maurice nodded and put his hands back to his head before leaning on his knees again. "I'll be right back."

Jamal left the waiting room and called Davidson.

"Davidson," he answered after the second ring.

"You still think Samir can be taken down by the book?" Jamal asked into his phone, angrily. "Because today shows he doesn't give a fuck. He attacked at a fucking funeral, my man!"

"I know Jamal, and I understand you're upset. You should be upset. But we can't just run around killing people because we think the world will be a better place without them. That's not up to us to decide," Davidson argued.

"You do what you gotta do. I'ma do what I gotta do. God bless my vest. Trying to do it your way could've gotten me killed today." Jamal disconnected

his call. He needed to move fast. Samir wasn't waiting.
He knew he couldn't either.

25

Ms. Keyona learned of the shooting that happened at Kiree's funeral and heard that Jamal had been shot. She scrambled for her phone and dialed his number. Jamal answered after the third ring.

"Williams," Jamal answered, not recognizing the number on his screen.

"JAMAL!" Ms. Keyona yelled. She burst into tears. "Oh my God! Are you okay? I heard you had been shot!"

"Mom, I'm fine. I had my vest on. I'm good. Ms. Niecie's niece Deisha was hit, though. She's Chanda's best friend. She was shot in her stomach and is in surgery," Jamal told his mom.

Ms. Keyona let out a sigh of relief. "Jamal, you said you were back in Philly for some unfinished business. I'm hearing rumors that you were assigned to the Philadelphia Police Department. Is this what I think this is about?"

Jamal waited a moment before saying anything. "Mom, I can't talk to you about this."

"Yes, it's police business. I understand that. But I can't help but wonder if this police business is really personal. And you know what happens when things get personal. Your judgment is clouded. You let your emotions lead you and you act without thinking. So I am telling you as your mother, don't let your personal vendetta against Samir cloud your judgment and cause you to act sloppy. It will get you killed." Ms. Keyona warned.

Jamal thought over what his mother said. He knew she was right but he didn't believe his judgment was cloudy. "I know mom. I hear you and I'm listening."

"I hope so. Stop by the house tonight. There's something I want to show you," Ms. Keyona said.

"I don't know if tonight will work mom, I have a lot to do."

"Tonight, Jamal. I mean it," his mother said firmly.

Jamal gave in. "Okay mom. I'll be there around 8 o'clock."

"Okay baby. I'll see you then. I love you."

"Love you too, mom." Jamal disconnected the call and closed his eyes. He looked back in the waiting room and saw that Maurice was gone. He walked over to the visitor's desk.

"Excuse me miss, I'm Detective Williams from the 22nd District. Has Deisha Burton gotten out of surgery?"

The nurse checked her computer. "Yes, she's been moved to room 318. A young man just went back."

"Thanks," Jamal said before walking away. He headed over to the room that Deisha was in and stood in the doorway. Maurice was sitting in a chair at her bedside holding her hand. Deisha had a tube in her mouth. He could tell she was sedated. Jamal had never seen Maurice look so hopeless. He imagined Maurice thought the same thing about him when he lost Tamera.

Jamal gently tapped on the door. Maurice looked up at him and then came to the doorway.

"We're still meeting tomorrow at my hotel room so we can work out the details for what we're trying to do. Are you still in?" Jamal asked Maurice.

"After what happened today, do you really need to ask me that?" Maurice replied as he looked at Jamal with tired eyes.

Jamal looked at Deisha and sighed deeply. "10am tomorrow, be at my hotel room. Samir will be at his warehouse around 1. We're moving on his ass then." Maurice had no words. He looked at Deisha also and then held his hand out to Jamal. Jamal took it and held it firmly. He then left and went back to his hotel room.

An hour after Jamal was settled in and awaiting his room service, his phone rang. He didn't recognize the number again and started to ignore the call but decided to answer it at the last minute.

"Williams," Jamal answered as he turned the television to ESPN.

"Jamal, what the fuck is going on?" a male voice boomed on the other end of the phone.

Jamal frowned. "Who the hell is this?"

"It's your brother. It's been that long since we talked on the phone that you forgot my voice?" Shawn asked.

Jamal looked at his watch and saw that it was after 6pm which meant it was after midnight over in Italy. "It's kinda late for you, homie. Shouldn't you be sleeping so you can hit the gym in the morning?" Jamal asked.

"Nah, we're off for the next two weeks. Don't try to change the subject. What's going on back home? The last time we talked, Kiree was killed, Manny was shot, and D-Ball was blowing niggas away and you were back in Philly. I just got finished on Skype with mommy and she told me you got shot earlier but luckily, you had your vest on. And now you're with the Philly Police Department. Something's up and I need to know what. Does this have anything to do with why you didn't want me to come back to Philly for Thanksgiving?" Shawn had a million and one questions and did not appreciate being left out of the loop.

"It's a lot going on right now. Too much for me to even get into." Jamal started.

"I have time. Talk to me, yo." Shawn said interrupting him.

Jamal sighed and began telling Shawn everything that happened from the phone call he got from Maurice asking him to come to Philly, to the ambush at Keisha's apartment and how she killed one of the gunmen. He then told Shawn how Keisha was raped in her holding cell and how Samir came after him. He told of the cop Davidson and how he had uncovered what really happened with Khalil as well as all of the corrupt cops on the force and the ones who were being killed to keep information from leaking about the dirty cops and their underhanded drug businesses. He also told Shawn that their father was an informant for the 22nd District which is what ultimately lead to Samir killing him. Lastly, he told his brother how he, Maurice, D-Ball and Manny were planning to take down Samir the following day and that they were ambushed again outside of Kiree and Ms. Becky's funeral. He did confirm that he had been shot but told his brother that fortunately, he had his vest on.

"So that's pretty much what's been going on right now. I didn't want you to come back to Philly because I know this shit is deep and I know Samir is gunning for me and D-Ball. And Keisha…man. Maurice little sister is a fucking rider."

"Why'd you say that?" Shawn asked as he grabbed a duffle bag and started packing some clothes. He didn't give a shit what Jamal said; he was coming home. He would rather be in Philly and have his brother's back than be all the way on the other side of the world and have to fly back home for Jamal's funeral.

"Because she shoots first and asks questions later. The way she snatched D-Ball's gun from out the back of his pants and started bussing shots, shit, I'm ready to ask if she ever thought of being a cop. Her aim is quick, too. She popped one dude twice in the chest and shot another in the stomach."

Shawn winced. "Got damn! Who the fuck taught her how to shoot like that?" he asked.

"Manny and D-Ball."

"That's crazy. Chanda was supposed to Skype with Deisha tonight but I guess I took too long with mom because she fell asleep," Shawn said as he looked at Chanda sleeping in their bed.

Jamal hesitated for a moment. "Deisha's in the hospital."

"For what? Is she okay?" Shawn asked.

"She got hit earlier when we were ambushed outside of the funeral. When we were inside, she said she noticed a guy that came in and viewed Kiree's body as if he was checking to make sure he was dead. Then she said the way he looked at me and Manny was like he was making sure it was us. When we got outside, she spotted him and pointed him out to me. In all the madness, I guess she didn't duck fast enough because when things started calming down, that's when Maurice noticed she was on the ground bleeding." Jamal shook his head as he thought of Tamera.

"Yo, this is fucking crazy! Samir is outta fucking control! That nigga got no picks. What the fuck made you wanna go up against him? Why you ain't just stay in Delaware and off his radar?" Shawn asked.

"Because I'm tired of this shit. I think he's wreaked enough havoc in the neighborhood and he needs to be stopped," Jamal explained.

Shawn packed up a few more of his things. "I can dig it. Listen, I just wanted to check in on you and make sure you were good. I can't have anything happening to my kids' uncle before they get the chance to know you."

"How about that? How are Amber and Andre?" Jamal asked as he threw on a shirt. He saw that it was almost the time for him to head to his mother's house so he could see whatever it was that she wanted to show him.

"They're doing well. They love it here. I think Amber is going to be a tomboy and Andre is heavy into drawing and coloring," Shawn told his brother.

"That's what's up. Well look, I'ma head over to mommy's real quick. I'ma holler at you later on. Kiss my niece and nephew for me and tell Chanda I said what's up."

"I will, yo." Jamal disconnected the call and checked to make sure he had everything. He then took his shirt off and put another vest on. He wasn't trying to get caught slipping. He checked his gun to make sure it was fully loaded and grabbed an extra clip just to be safe. He then grabbed his keys and his cell phone and left out to visit his mother.

26

Chanda stirred in her sleep and then woke up. She stretched before looking at Shawn. She saw the duffle bag and sat up.

"Umm…what's all this? Are you going somewhere?" she asked.

Shawn stood in front of the dresser with his back to her and took a deep breath. He was hoping what he was about to say to her didn't turn into an argument.

"I have to go back to Philly," he said in a low tone.

"For what? I thought you said Jamal told us to stay in Italy. Why are we going now? Is he finished whatever it is that he was doing?"

"We're not going to Philly. I am," Shawn said as he turned and faced her.

Chanda sat all of the way up in the bed and looked at Shawn as if he had lost his mind. "What the hell do you mean, you're going? You're just going to sneak off to Philly and leave us here without saying anything to me?"

"Babe, chill. Nobody is sneaking anywhere," Shawn replied.

Chanda pointed to the duffle bag. "Then what do you call this? Looks like you're trying to sneak off in the middle of the night. What were you going to do; leave a note on the nightstand?" Chanda was getting upset.

"Chanda, listen to me. I wasn't going to sneak off. I was going to let you know that I need to go back home. I just didn't want you to worry," Shawn said as he knelt in front of her.

"How can I not worry? Something is going on in Philly that brought Jamal back and now you're talking about joining him. I don't like how this sounds and I don't like the idea of us being separated from you here in Italy while you're all the way over in Philly. Is Jamal in trouble?" Chanda asked.

"I wouldn't say it's trouble. But I need to be there to back him up." Shawn was being evasive because he didn't want Chanda to worry.

"Shawn, I don't like this. You promised that you weren't getting involved with Jamal and his crazy shit anymore after Tammy was killed. You promised when we had Andre that you would put us first," she reminded him as she placed a hand on his chest.

"And y'all do come first. But he's my brother, babe. I need to make sure he's okay. I need to be there to back him up."

"What aren't you telling me?" Chanda asked as she searched Shawn's face.

Shawn looked down and hesitated before answering her. "Everything that you don't need to know."

"That's not good enough," Chanda said as she tilted Shawn's chin so he could look at her. "If you go, we're coming with you."

"No," Shawn said firmly. "No. I do not want my kids around this. You stay here until I either send for you, or I come back home. You and my kids are to stay here, I'm not playing. I've never tried to control you or force you to do anything you didn't want to do. But this time I am. I need you to listen to me and do what I say. Stay here."

Chanda stared at Shawn for a moment and then finally gave in. He cupped her face in the palm of his hands and gave her a kiss.

"I love you. And I love our kids. Y'all are my life."

"We know. And we love you, too. Just promise me that you will be safe and that you will either send for me, or come back home. Promise me that if it looks like it's too big for you and Jamal to handle that you will come back home. Promise me, Shawn." Chanda pleaded.

"I promise," Shawn said as he kissed her again. He then stood up and grabbed his iPad. He was able to book a flight to Philly that was leaving in two hours. That would get him into the city by 5am. He made sure he had everything and then called a cab. While he waited, he went into his children's room and watched them sleep for a moment before kissing each of them. He then went back to his bedroom and pulled Chanda up. He wrapped his arms around her and held her tight.

"I love you so much," Shawn told her.

"I love you too, baby." Chanda said in return.

Shawn kissed her and began to sway her from side to side. "Your name is going to look so good with Williams on the end."

Chanda laughed out loud. She kissed him just as the cab beeped its horn from outside. Chanda held onto him tightly not wanting to let him go. "Be careful," she said with her eyes closed.

"I will." Shawn kissed her longingly and she walked him to the door holding his hand. "I love you," he told her again.

"I love you," Chanda said as he let her hand go. Shawn tossed his bag in the back seat. Before he had a chance to get into the cab, a couple walked over to him and asked him for his autograph. He quickly gave it to them and then waved to Chanda before hopping inside of the cab. It sped off into the darkness and Shawn made his way back to Philly.

27

Jamal made his way over to his mother's house. She had just finished cooking pepper steak and rice with string beans and gravy. Though Jamal had already eaten, the smell of his mother's food awakened a hunger inside of him so he did not decline a plate when she offered.

As Jamal sat at the table enjoying the good meal, his mother pulled up a chair beside him and opened a photo album that Jamal had never seen before. Jamal stuck a spoonful of pepper steak and rice in his mouth before sipping on the cold Pepsi that Ms. Keyona had given to him as well.

"What are these?" Jamal asked as he wiped his mouth on a napkin.

"These," Ms. Keyona started as she turned a couple of pages, "are pictures from a long time ago. And this is your father; Andre Williams."

Jamal stared at the book and looked at the photo of his father. He looked like an 80's version of Jamal; same height, same build, same skin complexion. He listened to his mother as she flipped through the pages and pointed out the people in the photos. She shared memories with her son and short stories, telling him what was happening around the time the photos were taken. There was a photo of Andre holding Jamal when he was a baby. Andre looked like a proud father in the photo. There was another photo of Jamal holding his father's leg while he had Shawn on his shoulders. Ms. Keyona told him the photo was from Easter of 1986. One of the last photos that she had of Andre with them was of him holding Shawn up to a basketball hoop. It looked as if Shawn was dunking. The last photo was of Ms. Keyona and Andre. He was standing behind her with one arm around her waist and the other arm casually around her neck. Ms. Keyona looked as though she was glowing in the photo. She said it had been taken two weeks before he was killed.

"I don't doubt in my mind that he would have made an awesome father. Actually, he already was an awesome father. He loved and protected us with everything he had, down to his last day." Ms. Keyona stopped talking as she thought of her long lost love. She wiped her eyes before giving the tears a chance to fall.

"How come you never showed us this album?" Jamal asked.

"Well, I didn't want you to start asking questions that I couldn't answer. I went about all of this the wrong way," Ms. Keyona replied.

"Well you didn't have much of a choice, all things considered."

"Yeah. I thought I was doing what was best for you and Shawn but really, I was just being a coward."

"No mom. You were just doing what a mother does; protecting her kids. I don't blame you for what happened to our father. Samir earned that blame and I don't care what it takes, he's going to pay for it," Jamal said disdainfully. He took the photo album and looked at the first photo of his father. He wished like hell he could remember something about him. He wished he had been alive to help raise him and teach him to be a better man than he was. Ms. Keyona stared at her son wondering what he was thinking at that moment.

Jamal closed the photo album and finished his food in silence. He thought over what was supposed to happen the following day. He knew what he was trying to accomplish was dangerous and could possibly get him killed. But he swore he would try his hardest to take Samir with him. If he lived, Samir died. It was as simple as that.

When he was finished eating, he emptied his plate, washed it and put it away. He then went upstairs to his old bedroom and looked around. His mother had transformed it into a sitting room complete with a small futon, office desk, and leather office chair. An HP desktop computer sat on top with a printer and fax machine next to it. Adjacent to that was a small TV stand with a 32 inch flat screen TV on top. He looked on the wall and noticed only his graduation picture was hanging up there. He smiled to himself thinking that his mother still made sure it was "his" room. He left out and went to Shawn's room which had not changed much. His posters of Michael Jordan, Julius "Dr. J" Erving, Allen Iverson and Kobe Bryant were still on his wall. Some of his championship trophies and medals adorned his dressers. He picked up a picture that he saw leaning against one of the trophies.

"Damn, talk about a throwback." Jamal said aloud. It was a photo of Shawn, Jamal, Maurice and Raheem at their 8th grade class trip to the Poconos. He fixed his eyes on Raheem and chuckled at his mischievous grin. His life had changed so much since Raheem was murdered. He sat the picture back on the dresser and looked around before leaving the room and closing the door behind him. He went back downstairs and joined his mother in the kitchen as she was preparing to mop the floor.

"Mom," Jamal said. He lowered his eyes and shook his head as he thought of what he was about to say. "I just wanted to say that I know I didn't make it easy for you to raise me and Shawn. I wasn't rebelling because of you or because Dad wasn't around. I was just really lost and angry. But I want you to know I'm grateful for all of the sacrifices you made for me and Shawn; all of the times you came and bailed me out of jail. If I never get to say it, thanks for not giving up on me."

Ms. Keyona squeezed the water from her mop and looked at her son. "Jamal, you are more than welcome." Jamal lowered his eyes again feeling a knot in his stomach. "Are you sure everything is okay?" she asked her son.

"Everything is fine, mom." He walked over to her and gave her a kiss on the cheek. "Just know that I love you. I need to head back to my hotel room. I have a big day tomorrow and I better get some sleep. I'll lock the door behind me and call you when I get in." Jamal left out before his mother could ask any more questions and went back to his hotel room.

28

Shawn touched down in Philly a little after 5am. He checked into a hotel at the airport but only took a brief nap to shake off the jet-lag. When he woke up around 8:30am, he checked in with Chanda letting her know that he was back in Philly and was on his way to Jamal. He promised to check in every hour with her and the kids.

Shawn wasn't sure where he should stop first. He knew if he showed up at his mother's house, she would more than likely tell Jamal that he was there. He didn't want to give his brother the opportunity to try to stop him. He remembered that Jamal said Deisha had been shot. More than likely she was at Temple Hospital. He called over and confirmed that she was there. Shawn was willing to bet that Maurice was there, having never left her side. He rented a car and drove over to the hospital. When he arrived at Deisha's room, Maurice was in a chair with a blanket over him, sleeping. He looked at Deisha and was saddened to see her in the condition that she was in. Maurice stirred in the chair and woke up. He saw Shawn and looked at him wide eyed with surprise.

"What's up, yo?" Maurice spoke as he stood up to stretch. Shawn came into the room and shook Maurice's hand before hugging him. "When did you get back?"

"Around five this morning. How's Deisha?" Shawn asked.

Maurice sighed. "She's still out of it. They have her on a morphine drip for the pain. Getting shot in the stomach has to be one of the worse places to get hit."

"Damn," was all that Shawn could think to say.

"Where are Chanda and the kids?"

"I left them in Italy. I know what's supposed to go down today. That's why I'm here. I'm not about to let Jamal do this alone." Shawn said.

"He won't be alone. He got us as back up," Maurice assured him.

"Yeah, but he's my brother. I can't let him do this without me."

"You know Jamal ain't trying to hear that shit," Maurice said as he sat back down.

"Yeah well, we ain't kids anymore. Jamal can't stop me this time," Shawn said with defiance.

They talked for a little while until the doctors came in to check Deisha's vitals and run more tests.

Yani

She was still unconscious and didn't appear to be waking up anytime soon with the heavy medication they had her on. Maurice looked at his watch and saw that it was 9:30am. He ran his fingers through Deisha's hair and kissed her forehead.

"You stay strong for me, babe. I love you." Maurice said in Deisha's ear. He kissed her on her forehead again, this time lingering a little longer with his eyes closed. He and Shawn left and headed straight to Jamal's hotel room.

D-Ball and Manny were already at Jamal's when Maurice knocked on the door. Shawn stood off to the side so Jamal couldn't see him when he looked through the peephole. Jamal opened the door and was about to shake Maurice's hand when he saw Shawn standing next to him. His mouth hung open.

"No the fuck you didn't," Jamal said to his younger brother.

"Yes the fuck I did. Now are you going to let me in or stand there undressing me with your eyes?" Shawn asked with sarcasm.

Jamal couldn't help laughing. He slapped his brother a handshake and hugged him. They came inside and Manny and D-Ball gave Shawn handshakes and hugs welcoming him there.

"Not cool, Shawn. I told you to stay in Italy. I didn't want you caught up in this."

"Yeah well, you got shot yesterday. And if it wasn't for that vest, I would've had to come back and help Mommy bury you. That shit ain't gonna fly. I know you got back up, but ain't no fucking back up like having your brother here. So save the bitching until this is over," Shawn said firmly.

Jamal had no argument. He knew how it was once Shawn made his mind up. But he still didn't like the idea of his younger brother being in the line of fire especially since he had two kids to take care of.

They sat down and began discussing the plan. Jamal didn't tell Davidson what the plan was because he didn't want to be talked out of it. D-Ball sat loading all of the guns and putting bullets in clips as Jamal talked to them. Maurice and Manny put on the vests that Jamal had for them. Jamal looked at Shawn and shook his head.

"Yeah, you're definitely not going now. I don't have a vest for you," Jamal said figuring that would keep Shawn from getting involved.

"Jamal, stop it. Vest or no vest, I'm coming," Shawn said adamantly.

Jamal stared at Shawn annoyed with his defiance. He shook his head and took his vest off. "Put this on," he said to Shawn as he handed it to him. "Don't argue with me about this shit either, Shawn. You wanna be down, you do this shit my way and how I say. This ain't a fucking game."

"What about you, 'Mal?" Shawn asked as he pulled his shirt over his head and put the vest on.

Jamal looked at D-Ball. "Back me up in there."

"You know it," D-Ball replied as he loaded his guns and put them both in the small of his back. He had a third gun with him that he had in an ankle holster. He passed a gun and an extra clip to Maurice and passed another to Manny. Lastly, he passed one to Shawn. He looked at Shawn with a smirk on his face. "Aim and squeeze; shoot to kill. Sounds simple, doesn't it?" D-Ball asked him.

Shawn took a deep breath. "Yeah, it does."

"Well it ain't. You need to listen to your brother. It takes more than just aiming and squeezing a trigger. You either gotta be trained to kill or heartless enough to kill. You ain't neither." D-Ball schooled Shawn.

Jamal looked at D-Ball and Shawn but didn't say anything. He heard a knock at his door and signaled for everyone to put their weapons away. He looked out the peep-hole and saw that it was Detective Davidson. He shook his head and opened the door.

"You really need to keep your ringer on your phone, homie," Davidson said as he came in. He looked around at everyone suspiciously. He could tell something was going on. He definitely knew something was up when he saw Shawn standing in a corner.

"Well, if it ain't Italiano's finest; Shawn Williams. Give me two guesses why you're back in town. But I bet money I'm only going to need one," Davidson said with a smirk on his face.

"Just here to see my family for the holidays," Shawn lied with a smile.

"Yeah, bullshit." Davidson chuckled. "Listen Jamal, we gotta roll. Judge just signed off on a warrant to that warehouse you said Samir took you to. That cop that assaulted Keisha is singing like a bitch over in his hospital room. We have two uniforms guarding him. But we can nail Samir's punk ass today."

Jamal frowned and shook his head. Davidson had just thrown a serious monkey wrench into his plans. He looked at Manny, Maurice, Shawn and D-Ball as they all looked at him wondering what he was going to do. He thought of what his mother said about letting his personal vendetta with Samir cloud his better judgment and decided at that moment that he would do it Davidson's way. If he could take down Samir legally without any of his friends being killed or his brother getting hurt, he was going to do it.

Jamal took a deep breath and grabbed his coat. "Let's do it." He shook Davidson's hand. "I'll meet you down in your car in a minute." Davidson left and closed the door behind him. Jamal put his hands on the door and hung his head.

"Now what, 'Mal?" Manny asked. "Because even though your little cop friend has a warrant, I don't think Samir is going to come willingly."

"Fucking right on that shit." D-Ball agreed.

"D-Ball, come here." Jamal said as he stepped out into the hallway. D-Ball followed behind him.

"Of everybody in there, you're the only one that I know has a clear head. Maurice is fucked up over Deisha, Manny is fucked up over Keisha, Kiree and his mom not to mention he just got shot. And Shawn…he ain't built like that. Davidson won't let you come with us. But I need you to come. If anything goes down, I need you at my back. Can you do this?" Jamal asked his friend.

"I got you," D-Ball said as he slapped Jamal a firm handshake. Jamal didn't have the heart to say good-bye to his brother or friends so he left and went straight to

Davidson's car. They got in and left out to meet up with the other cops who were executing the warrant for Samir.

D-Ball went back into Jamal's hotel room and sat down quietly. Shawn and the others looked at him waiting for him to say something.

"So…what now?" Shawn asked.

D-Ball didn't respond right away. "What now? Maurice goes back to the hospital with Deisha. Manny goes home to his son and Keisha and Shawn…go visit your mom."

"And you?" Maurice asked D-Ball, having a feeling that something was up.

D-Ball shrugged with a smirk on his face. "Don't worry about me. Y'all go do y'all thing. Jamal asked me to lock up." They looked at D-Ball suspiciously but didn't know what else to do so they left. D-Ball then realized that Jamal didn't put his vest back on. He left the hotel room and jumped into his car so he could head over to the warehouse.

29

Jamal rode over to the warehouse with Davidson in silence. While Davidson could barely contain his excitement, Jamal didn't have a good feeling. A text message came through on his phone from D-Ball letting him know he was right behind them. Shortly after, a call came through on Davidson's phone.

"Davidson," he answered as he stopped his car on the corner of the block where the warehouse was located. Davidson listened as the person on the other end of the phone informed him that the cop who was being guarded at the hospital had been killed. Davidson beat his fist on the steering wheel. "Got damn it, sonuva bitch!" Jamal looked at him wondering what happened to set him off. "How the fuck did this happen? You find out how the security detail broke down and get me some fucking information right now!" he fumed before disconnecting the call.

"What happened?" Jamal asked.

Davidson waited a moment before speaking. "The cop that was going to give a statement and testify against Samir was killed this morning. The two cops who were supposed to relieve the original ones on the security detail weren't the actual cops assigned to him. One bullet to the head and they were long gone before the actual cops who were supposed to be guarding him arrived." Davidson was clearly pissed.

"What the fuck?" Jamal said with his mouth hanging open. "So now what? With no witness, how the hell are we supposed to bring Samir down?" Jamal asked. This was already starting to go bad.

"We still execute the warrant. No sense in wasting it. Who knows; maybe we can wear him down at the precinct."

"I don't know. Maybe we should hold off until we can get something solid," Jamal suggested.

"Why are you trying to back out, Jamal? I thought you wanted this," Davidson was confused.

"Yes, I want this. But something just doesn't feel right."

"Look, it's real simple. We have a warrant. We go in, grab the bastard and take him to the station. Simple as that." Davidson got out of the car. Jamal hesitated as he played with Tamera's ring around his neck. He kissed it and tucked it inside of his shirt before getting out of the car and following Davidson over to the warehouse. Jamal drew his gun when they got to the doors. Davidson pounded on it with his fist. "Police, we have a warrant!" he yelled through the door. When no one answered, he drew his gun as well and kicked the door in. Two uniformed officers were behind them. Davidson moved in and pointed his gun to the right. Jamal pointed his to the left and then looked up. It was quiet; too quiet. Jamal didn't like that. Not only was it quiet, but a wide open space which was perfect for an ambush. Not too many places to duck behind and not too many places to hide.

Jamal kept his gun drawn and continued looking around. He was just about to put his gun down when the uniformed officer behind him was shot.

Jamal ducked and scrambled for a wall to hide behind. Davidson did the same. The other uniform didn't move fast enough and he was shot twice before falling to the ground.

"Sonuva bitch!" Davidson screamed. "Where the fuck are they coming from?"

"I don't know," Jamal yelled back to him. He peeked from behind the wall and looked up. It was dark and he couldn't see much. He was leaning out too far and shots rang out in his direction. He jumped back some. There were four gunmen. Two began moving in Jamal's direction and the other two moved in Davidson's direction. Davidson fired at them but missed. Jamal fired and caught one in the groin and in the chest. The other three fired excessively. Jamal waited until they stopped to reload and jumped up to fire at them. He caught one but missed the other. He ran and dove behind a set of stairs. *"Where the fuck is D-Ball?"* Jamal thought to himself as he dumped the empty clip and slammed a full one inside of his gun. More shots rang out. He waited a moment when it got quiet.

"You good, Keith!" Jamal yelled out.

"Yeah. The other two are down." He radioed for back up. Jamal came from behind the stairs and tucked his gun in the small of his back. Davidson was putting his radio in his coat pocket when he saw someone move in the shadows behind Jamal.

"Jamal!" Davidson yelled out. Jamal turned around too slow. Davidson grabbed him, trying to knock him to the ground when more shots rang out. Jamal was missed but Davidson was hit five times in the back and in his leg. He collapsed on top of Jamal.

Jamal struggled to move from under Davidson so he could pull his gun but he was stuck. His heart raced as he saw the gunman emerge from the shadows. He couldn't believe it was about to end this way. He braced himself for whatever was about to happen next when he heard a loud boom. The gunman arched his back and dropped his gun. The loud, roaring boom sounded off again hitting the gunman in his back and exiting his chest. He dropped to the ground face down.

D-Ball was standing behind him holding his Desert Eagle. Jamal looked up at D-Ball breathing heavy. He thanked God for the save but immediately turned his attention to Davidson.

"Oh naw, man. Naw!" Jamal yelled. He searched Davidson's coat pocket for his radio after finally being able to sit up. "I need back up, now!" Jamal screamed into it. He rattled off the address. "Officers down! OFFICERS DOWN!!" Jamal held Davidson tight after turning him over. "Stay with me man, hang in there. Don't you fucking quit! Stay with me!" Jamal yelled as he trembled. He grabbed the radio again. "Somebody send some help, I've got an officer down, NOW!!"

D-Ball knelt next to them. "He's gone, 'Mal," D-Ball said to him. "He's gone."

Jamal looked at D-Ball and then looked at Davidson who stared up at the ceiling with lifeless eyes. It was just like looking down at Raheem many years before when he died in his arms. Jamal closed his eyes and sighed deeply. He shook his head and closed Davidson's eyes before laying him on the ground so he could stand up.

"Was Samir here?" Jamal asked D-Ball.

"No. Nobody was upstairs or in the back. They knew y'all were coming. This was a set-up and y'all walked right into it."

"Unbelievable," Jamal mumbled as he shook his head. "Un-fucking-believable." He threw the radio into a wall and kicked open the door just as more cops were pulling up and storming the place.

Jamal walked over to Davidson's car and leaned on it. He put his hands to his face as the tears fell. Though he didn't know Davidson that well, Jamal knew that he was a good man; a good man who reached out to him all the way in Delaware so he could help take down Samir; a good man who honored his badge above everything else; a good man who had put his life on the line to save Jamal's. And now he was dead. If only Davidson had listened to him and did things Jamal's way, he might still be alive. Jamal thought back to what D-Ball said; it was an ambush, they knew Jamal and Davidson were coming. Someone tipped them off. But who?

Despite how devastated Jamal was over what happened, he cooperated with the police and assisted with the investigation. There were no drugs in the warehouse, nothing that could further extend the warrant for Samir's arrest. There was no way Jamal could prove that Samir set up the ambush that left one officer dead and two critically injured. And with the other cop dead who agreed to testify against Samir, there was nothing they could do from that end either. The warehouse wasn't even in Samir's name; it was linked to the same officer who was now in the morgue with a bullet wound to the head. Basically, they were right back where they started in the beginning. No evidence, no witnesses, and Samir was a free man still walking the streets.

Jamal went back to the police station and began packing the few things he had at his desk. With the case hitting a brick wall and Davidson dead, there was no reason for him to stay. He was going back home. He noticed he had a few notes on his desk from Davidson letting him know he was trying to get in touch with him about the warrant. He had a hunch to check his voicemail. Jamal listened to the messages and one from Davidson in particular caught his attention.

"Hey Jamal. This is Davidson. Man you really suck with answering your phone. The cop that assaulted Keisha is singing like a bitch right now and is ready to make a deal. He gave us some information about the warehouse that you were taken to. Now, I just got the warrant from Judge Carlisle and we're moving on Samir this afternoon to take him in. We're finally gonna nail this sonuva bitch. Since we still don't know who's on

what side, I'm keeping a tight lid on this. The only one who knows specifically who the warrant is for and what it's about is Jessica Armstrong. She's good people. So if you get this message and can't get in touch with me, check in with her and she'll give you the details. If I don't hear from you in the next hour, I'm coming to your hotel room so we can handle this. Alright Jamal, peace!"

Jamal played the message again and wrote Jessica's name down. He had crossed paths with Jessica once or twice. He never thought twice about her because she seemed eager to help. Now it was dawning on him that she was too eager. She was the one who tipped Samir off. He looked over at her at her desk with her fake tears of remorse and sorrow.

"Snaky bitch," Jamal said to himself. He stared at her for a long time thinking whether or not he should blow the whistle on her ass or follow his original thought and take his ass back to Delaware. He had no wins against Samir. He got lucky three times. He didn't want to take a chance with Lady Luck a fourth time.

Jamal made sure he saved the message and grabbed his box to leave. He placed his box in the trunk of his car and slammed it shut when he felt a gun pressed against his head.

"Don't even think about it," he heard a female voice say. "Put your hands up Jamal, like a good boy and I won't turn you into a statistic in the Daily News." The voice was familiar but he needed to see the face to believe it. He felt her hand search him and pull his gun from his waist. She then pushed him into the car. "You can turn around now," she said seductively.

Jamal turned around slowly and faced the female holding the gun. He looked at her in shock unable to believe his eyes.

"What's the matter, baby? You look like you've seen a ghost," she said to him with a slight grin.

Jamal shook his head. "Kareema…?"

"I love it when you say my name," she motioned with her gun for him to get into the Black Buick Lacrosse that was next to them. When the door opened, Samir was sitting in the back seat. Jamal climbed in the car hesitantly wondering if things could possibly get any worse.

30

Jamal rode around with Samir for a long time. At first, Jamal thought he was going to be taken some place specific. Then Jamal had an idea that Samir was driving him around aimlessly to make sure he didn't have a tail before he reached his final destination. Jamal was nervous. He hadn't checked in with Shawn or his mother. He had no back up, no gun and couldn't think of a way to get himself out of whatever he was about to get into. Judging by the previous attempts Samir made on his life, he was absolutely positive that Samir intended to kill him.

Jamal put his hands in his pockets and felt his phone. He wished he was able to make a phone call to someone to let them know where he was. He then had an idea. His Galaxy S II had GPS tracking. He closed his eyes to get an image of what his phone looked like. Using his thumb, he moved it along the side of the phone until he found the power button. He knew his ringer was off as he thought back to Davidson's message reminding Jamal to keep his ringer on. He moved his finger along the face of the screen hoping that he was pulling the top menu down. *'First button wifi; second, Bluetooth; third, GPS.*" He moved his finger over the top of the screen and prayed that he tapped the right button for the GPS to cut on. He then moved his finger around the face of his phone and tried to visualize what it looked like. He pressed the phone button and tapped his last contact which was Maurice. He prayed that Maurice picked up.

Maurice was back at the hospital with Shawn. Deisha was still heavily medicated and unconscious. He was holding her hand with his head down when his phone rang. He saw it was Jamal and answered.

"Yo homie, what's good?" Maurice answered. When he didn't receive a response he said hello louder. He then looked at his phone with a puzzled face.

"What?" Shawn asked, looking up from his phone as he was messaging Chanda on Facebook.

"It's Jamal but he's not saying anything," Maurice said.

"Hang up, he probably called by accident," Shawn replied, being dismissive.

Maurice put the phone back to his ear and listened. He could hear muffling noises and was about to hang up and call Jamal back when he heard his voice.

"Samir, you been driving me around for over a half hour. Are you gonna kill me or are we just going to do some site seeing?"

"Oh shit!!" Maurice exclaimed.

"What?" Shawn asked as he looked up at him.

"Samir's got Jamal," Maurice said as he looked at Shawn.

"What!" Shawn snapped as he jumped from his chair.

Maurice put it on speaker phone. They listened to the conversation between Jamal and Samir as their hearts raced.

"Jamal!" Shawn said loudly.

"Shhh!!" Maurice said as he held up a finger.

"Don't fucking shush me! This muthafucka got my brother and you talking about some shush! JAMAL!" Shawn yelled again.

"Shawn, shut up! Jamal didn't call us by accident. You honestly think Samir knows Jamal has one of us let alone both of us on his phone?" Maurice said angrily.

"So what the fuck are you saying?" Shawn asked almost panicking.

"He probably called on a sneak tip to let us know what's up. Give me your phone and keep listening to hear if Jamal says where he is."

Shawn gave Maurice his phone. "Who are you calling?"

"D-Ball and Manny," Maurice replied as he dialed D-Ball's number. Shawn continued to listen.

"Why the fuck are we all the way out Darby?" Jamal asked as he recognized a few of the streets. He still didn't know if he was able to get anybody on the phone nor was he certain of how much battery life he had. But he prayed like hell somebody was listening and recognized the call for what it was. *"Please don't hang up,"* he thought to himself.

"He's in Darby!" Shawn yelled to Maurice.

"D-Ball! We got a problem, yo. Samir has Jamal." Maurice said quickly when D-Ball answered.

D-Ball bolted from his seat. "You've gotta be fucking kidding me. Where?"

"Shawn just said they're in Darby. Jamal called my phone but he isn't on it. I don't think he did it by accident because we can hear him talking. We gotta move fast, yo!"

"Wait, wait, wait. Hold the fuck on. Where in Darby? That's too fucking vague."

"Shawn, did he say where?" Maurice asked.

"No, it's a lot of muffled noises. I barely hear Samir but Jamal hasn't said anything else yet." Shawn said. He had begun to pace. He prayed that he wasn't about to hear his brother's murder over the phone. "Wait, I can hear Jamal again, hold on."

"What is it with you and females, Sa'? Damn, you setting bitches up to get raped, you got my girl Kareema to set me up. You even used the cop chick Jessica Armstrong to set up me and Keith. How fucking grimy is that?" Jamal said with malice.

"What the fuck…?" Shawn said.

"What? What he say?"

"Jamal just said his girl Kareema set him up and some cop bitch named Jessica Armstrong set him and Keith up earlier," Shawn said as he continued to listen.

Maurice repeated what Shawn said back to D-Ball. "We don't have a lot of time, we gotta hurry up, yo." Maurice said as he grabbed his coat and his keys.

"What kind of phone does Jamal have?" D-Ball asked.

"He has a Galaxy S II, why?" Maurice asked, not sure what that had to do with anything.

"All Androids have GPS tracking. We might be able to find him that way."

"Yeah but how? Davidson is dead. We don't have any pull." Maurice replied.

"That bitch Jessica better start talking. I don't give a fuck if she is a female and a cop. Fuck that bitch; I got no picks right now. I'm not losing another one of my fucking homies to Samir's bitch-ass. Meet me at the police station. Hurry up because it ain't no telling how much time we got." D-Ball disconnected the call.

"What's going on?" Manny asked when he saw D-Ball tucking his gun in the back of his pants.

"Samir grabbed Jamal and has him somewhere out Darby. This shit is about to go down, we gotta roll," D-Ball told him as he handed Manny a gun. Keisha over heard what D-Ball said. "I'm coming with y'all."

"No, you stay here with my son," Manny told her as he put the safety on his gun and put it in the front of his pants.

"I can take Kamir to my mom's house or to Angie. I'm coming." Keisha insisted.

"Keisha, I'm not arguing with you about this shit, alright!" Manny said with base in his voice. "I get it, you're a rider. You've got my back. Now I need you to have my son's back and stay here. I'm not fucking asking you, I'm telling you."

Keisha froze for a moment. She decided to listen to Manny even though everything in her body screamed for her to go with him. She grabbed him and hugged him tightly. "You come home to me. You come home to me and our son. I'm not playing," Keisha said as she looked him in his eyes. Manny nodded and kissed her.

"Come on, Manny. Let's go!" D-Ball called to him as he headed for the front door. Manny left out behind D-Ball and they headed over to the precinct. Maurice and Shawn were already outside when they got there.

"He's still on the phone but they aren't saying much. I still hear muffling and some music from a car radio or something but that's it." Shawn told them.

"Okay, so what's the plan? How do we get this bitch Jessica to tell us where Jamal is?" Maurice asked D-Ball.

D-Ball looked at Shawn. "Mr. Superstar is going to go in there and get her."

"How the fuck am I supposed to do that?" Shawn asked.

"I don't know but you better think fast," D-Ball said. Shawn looked at all of them and shook his head. He walked in and went over to the help desk.

"Excuse me…" he started to say.

"Oh shit! I know who you are," the cop behind the desk said. Shawn looked at him confused. "You're Shawn Williams! You play for that basketball team Cimberio Varese!! I followed your career ever since you won the championship with University City High

School back in 2002! Wow!" the cop said with excitement.

Shawn was speechless and didn't know what to say as he was caught off guard.

"I've gotta get your autograph. My son plays basketball and he saw some of your games when you were a Hoya. He's gonna flip when I tell him I saw you," the cop said as he scrambled for a piece of paper and a pen. Shawn made the autograph out just as it was requested. The cop looked at it and then tucked it in his back pocket. "Are you looking for Jamal?"

"Actually no, I was hoping I could talk with a Jessica Armstrong." Shawn said nervously.

"Yeah, yeah Jessie is still here. We're all shook up over what happened out there earlier. Davidson was a good guy, great cop. I heard he saved your brother in that ambush earlier. Terrible. We're gonna get the sons of bitches who did this, mark my words. I hate to see Jamal leave, too. It was really good having him with us even if it was only temporarily. There's Jessie right now," the cop said as he spotted Jessica coming in his direction. "Jess, this is Shawn Williams, Jamal's younger brother. He plays basketball over in Italy." The cop introduced them as if he and Shawn had been the best of friends.

Jessica looked at Shawn, startled. She stuck out her hand to be shaken. "Hi, nice to meet you. I worked with your brother, briefly. It was a real pleasure." She looked away to avoid giving Shawn eye contact.

"Is it okay if I talk to you for a minute?" Shawn asked as he peered at her.

Jessica hesitated. "Sure, come over to my desk."

"Nice seeing you, Shawn!" the desk cop said with a huge smile on his face before he sat back down. Shawn waved to him before following Jessica over to her desk.

"What can I do for you?" Jessica asked as she tried hard to mask how nervous she was in front of Shawn. Shawn was nervous as well but decided to play Devil's Advocate to see if it would get him somewhere.

"Listen, I don't have a lot of time. I know Samir has you on his payroll. I know you tipped him off about the warrant my brother and Davidson were supposed to serve him today. Your tip got a cop killed and now Samir has my brother. Now I don't know if you've been paying attention lately, but Samir ain't biased when it comes to taking out women so don't think you're safe under his protection. And even if you are, that won't stop us from coming after you if

283

something happens to my brother," Shawn said in a low voice.

Jessica looked at him with a smirk on her face. "You've got a lot of nerve coming in here all cocky trying to threaten me. I guess you think you're bad because you went overseas to play ball. That doesn't mean shit to me. As far as I'm concerned, you and your brother are the same fucking thugs you were as kids and ain't shit changed except maybe your dick size and the hair on your face. I don't have to help you with shit."

"Samir is going to kill my brother. He had a friend of yours killed. What makes you any different than the thugs you claim we are when you're helping thugs commit murder? And you're supposed to be a cop?!"

"Go back to Italy, Shawn. It would be a shame for your mother to have to bury both of her sons and an even bigger shame if your children grew up fatherless like you and Jamal," Jessica said as she pretended to be gathering paper work to handle.

Shawn stared at her for a space of heartbeats before saying anything. "How long do you think Samir will let you live if I tell him you were passing information about him to your Lieutenant? If something happens to my brother because you didn't help me, I promise you, I might not be able to kill you personally but I'll gladly smile down on your corpse knowing I helped set you up the way you set my brother up, you bitch!" Shawn shook with fury as he looked at Jessica in disgust.

Jessica stared back at him to see if he was bluffing. She thought twice about his warning and knew what the consequences would be if Samir even thought someone was passing information off about him.

"He'll kill me either way," she whispered.

"Not if we get to him first. I'm not asking for you to come. I just need your help to find my brother."

Jessica took a deep breath and closed her eyes. Deep down she felt horrible about how things ended with Davidson because of the tip she gave Samir. She had feelings for Davidson and they sometimes flirted together though nothing ever came of it. Now she would never have the chance to see where things could have gone between them.

"What do you need me to do?" she asked Shawn.

Shawn let out a sigh of relief and quickly pulled Maurice's phone from his pocket. Thankfully Jamal was still on the line. "I need you to track Jamal using the GPS on his cell phone. Can you do that?" Shawn asked hastily. "We don't have a lot of time. Samir has been driving him around for probably an hour."

"Yeah, I can just trace this call." Jessica took the phone from Shawn and plugged it into her computer with a USB cable. She used a police program to tap the call. She pulled up a map where a flashing red dot pulsated on her screen as she waited for Jamal's destination to be revealed. Shawn tapped his foot as butterflies filled his stomach. Jessica typed quickly as she looked from the phone to the computer screen.

"Okay, his location is locked. He's near Darby Creek Trestle." She looked at the phone again. "Shit."

"What? What's wrong?" Shawn asked.

"The call dropped," Jessica said as she looked at Shawn.

"Fuck, what does that mean? Can we still track him?" Shawn asked.

"Yes, we can still track Jamal from the GPS on his phone as long as it stays on," Jessica told him.

Shawn snatched Maurice's phone. He then rattled his number to her. "Call my phone and keep tracking him, please." Shawn hurried from her desk and ran outside.

"What's going on?" Maurice asked.

"Jamal is near Darby Creek Trestle. But his call dropped. Jessica is still tracking him through his GPS. Let's move!" Shawn said as he hopped inside of his rental car. D-Ball turned to Manny and stopped him.

"What?" Manny asked.

"Go back home to Keisha and Kamir," D-Ball said to him.

"What?" Manny asked, confused. "Y'all can't do this without me."

"Listen, you and Keisha been through enough. You don't have anything else to prove. Go home and we'll handle this."

"D-Ball, let's move!" Maurice yelled from his car. Manny gave his best friend a firm handshake and stood back so D-Ball could get into his car. He pulled off and Maurice followed. Shawn honked his horn and stuck his hand out of the window letting them know to follow behind him once he had Jessica on the phone. They hauled ass to Jamal hoping they weren't too late.

31

Samir finally had Kareema stop the car on the side of a narrow passageway. Jamal looked around and saw nothing but trees. It was almost complete darkness. Jamal definitely didn't like the way this was looking. He tried to remain positive and told himself he was not going to beg for his life and he was not going to go down without a fight.

"Okay, so we finally stopped. Now what?" Jamal asked as he looked out of the window.

"Get out of the car," Samir told him.

"Man, you must be outta your fucking mind," Jamal said in a low voice. "This looks like a place to dump a fucking body and you ain't about to dump mine."

Samir laughed. "Yeah this is a nice place to dump a body. But I don't need to dump your body if you're already here. Now get the fuck out of the car," he ordered.

"What's the matter, Sa'? Scared to fuck up the upholstery?" Jamal chuckled as he stalled hoping to buy enough time to figure his way out of this. He still had his hand in his pocket.

Samir laughed with him. "Kareema?"

Before Jamal had a chance to brace himself, Kareema turned and shot him in his arm. Jamal hollered out in pain as he reached for his arm. The bullet from her .22 made his arm feel as though it was on fire. Samir laughed at him. Kareema got out of the car and walked around to Jamal's side before opening his door. Once she did, Samir used his foot to kick him out of the car. Jamal fell to the dirty ground grimacing in pain. He rolled over on his back and scooted against the car, using the door to help him stand up.

"You bitch," Jamal grimaced as he glared at Kareema.

Kareema gave him an evil grin. "Aww Mally, that wasn't nice, now was it?" She kneed him in his groin making him crouch over.

Samir got out of the car and leaned onto the hood. "It ain't shit for me to torch this fucking car, Jamal. So whether she kills you in it or right where your bitch-ass is kneeling, it don't make me no never mind. I just want your ass bodied."

"Wow, you went from hiding behind niggas, to hiding behind bitches," Jamal laughed. "Still don't have the balls to do shit yourself."

Yani

Kareema hit Jamal in his face with the butt of the gun and then pushed her heel in his chest as she aimed at him with both hands.

Samir shook his head. "You always were a disrespectful muthafucka, you know that?" he said to his cousin. "You don't look so fucking tough now, do you?"

"Fuck you," Jamal said before spitting blood onto the ground. He looked up at Kareema and shook his head at her.

"Don't be mad, Jamal. This is business, nothing personal." She moved her heel from his chest and shot him in his leg. Jamal yelled out in pain again as he fell to the ground. He couldn't believe he was going out like this. Why did it have to be slow? Why was Samir torturing him? He was losing hope for a rescue and slowly started to believe this was really the end of his line…

Just before Samir ordered Kareema to stop the car, Shawn was on the expressway with D-Ball and Maurice following behind him. They all were dipping from lane to lane trying to dodge the traffic and get to Jamal as quickly as possible.

"The tracking stopped," Jessica said to Shawn on the phone.

"What do you mean it stopped?" Shawn asked.

"I mean, they aren't moving anymore. Where ever Samir was taking Jamal, they're there."

"Where exactly is that?" Shawn asked as his heart raced. *"Please let me make it. Please,"* he thought to himself.

"They're still at Darby Creek Trestle. I can try to get a closer imaging based on the latitude and longitude of the GPS signal." Jessica was quiet for a moment as she waited. "I've got it. He's at the southeast end of the terrace not too far from the creek. Cut around the Sharon Hill Trolley line and you might be able to cut them off from there."

"Thanks Jessica," Shawn said.

"Don't thank me. Shawn, I'm sorry about what I said, and what I did. And I hope you get to Jamal in time," Jessica said quickly.

"Yeah, you and me both." Shawn disconnected the call and then called Maurice.

"Yo!" Maurice answered.

"Mar, Jamal is near the southeast end of Darby Creek Terrace. Jessica said to cut around the Sharon Hill Trolley line. Call D-Ball and tell him what I said. We gotta hurry the fuck up. I don't know how much longer we have." Shawn disconnected the call and strapped his seat belt on after getting off the next exit ramp and stopping at a red light. He looked in the glove compartment to make sure the gun was still in there. He remembered what D-Ball said to him earlier about either being trained to kill or heartless enough to kill. He agreed that he was neither, but he was willing to do what he had to do to save his brother. D-Ball pulled up to the right of him and signaled Shawn to let him know which direction he was going. When the light turned green, he sped off. Shawn checked his rear view mirror. He flashed his high beams at Maurice. Maurice flashed his back twice. Shawn took a deep breath and drove down the pathway that led to Darby Creek Trestle. His heart raced and his stomach was in knots as he feared the worst but hoped for the best.

D-Ball was the first on the scene. He turned his lights off and slowly drove around. He looked at the GPS on his phone to see if his latitude and longitude was close to where Shawn said Jamal was. He didn't need his phone any longer because he heard the gunshot.

"Shit," D-Ball said as he stopped the car. He got out and pulled both of his guns. He made sure he stayed in the shadows as he crept in the direction that the sound of the gunshot came from. He saw the black

Buick Lacrosse and dipped behind a tree. He peeped out to see what was going on and to get an idea of how many were out there. He was glad to see Jamal was alive but could tell that he had been shot by the way he was holding his arm. He saw Samir standing by the car and saw another guy standing near him. There were three of them and one of him. He wondered where the fuck Shawn and Maurice were. He aimed to see if he could get a clear shot of Samir just as Jamal was shot in his leg. D-Ball panicked and squeezed the trigger, missing Samir but catching his male partner in the neck. He cursed himself. Samir ducked and jumped behind a tree, pulling his own gun. Not wanting to be shot, Kareema grabbed Jamal and made him stand up. She put the gun to his neck as she stood behind him and backed towards a tree away from the shootout between D-Ball and Samir.

"I never would've guessed you would be so fucking heartless," Jamal said as he breathed heavy, in serious pain from the gunshot wounds to his leg and arm. "How the fuck did you get mixed up with that fucker, anyway?" he asked as he winced in pain.

"That's the least of your worries. But if you must know, Samir made one helluva deal with me that I couldn't refuse. He would make sure that my brother was taken care of in prison while he did his bid. He wouldn't have to worry about money, being traded for a pack of cigarettes or anything like that. All I had to do was keep an eye on you. I didn't think it was a big deal; until Samir started wanting more. He wanted me to smuggle drugs into the prisons. He has a few of the guards under his belt as well so it was nothing for me to get past metal detectors and searches. Until one day I was searched. But it wasn't your ordinary search. The pig bastard forced me to suck his nasty dick and Samir told me he could have a lot worse done to my brother if I did not show up today to help him kill you. I am my brother's keeper, which makes you expendable."

Jamal was pissed. He swore if he could he would whip her fucking ass like a man.

D-Ball was out of bullets and so was Samir. Shawn and Maurice arrived but Maurice did not have his gun.

"Looks like we got ourselves a situation here," Samir said as he peeked from behind the tree that was shielding him. "Kareema, where's my little cousin?" he called out.

Kareema eased forward into the light. Shawn looked at her and then looked at Samir. He pointed his gun at Kareema.

"Oh you done fucked up today, bitch," Shawn said coldly.

"Oh no, you've got it all wrong. You're the one who has it fucked up," Kareema said. "Let Samir go and I won't kill your brother."

"Bitch, you're crazy." Maurice said as he looked from Kareema to Samir.

"Not hardly," Kareema said as she chambered a round. "I've already shot your brother twice. All it takes is one more bullet in the right place. Now who's more important, your brother or your cousin?"

Shawn kept his gun aimed in Jamal and Kareema's direction without saying anything.

Samir laughed as he hopped inside of the Buick Lacrosse and drove off. D-Ball cursed, pissed that they missed an opportunity to finally take Samir out. He regretted making Manny stay home thinking an extra gunman could have helped and was pissed that Maurice left his gun in the car.

"Shoot that bitch, Shawn." D-Ball said furiously, wanting someone to die tonight to pay for all of the madness they'd endured over the last couple of weeks.

"Let him go, Kareema. You don't want to do this," Shawn said, ignoring D-Ball's request.

"No, you put your gun down and I'll walk away willingly. And your brother lives to fight another day."

"Fuck that, Shawn. Shoot her!" Jamal said as he looked at his younger brother.

"She's a female," Shawn said with hesitation.

"Correction, I'm a bitch with a gun. Drop yours or my trigger finger might get a little happy," Kareema threatened.

"Give me the fucking gun, I'll shoot that bitch." D-Ball practically growled.

"Drop your gun, Shawn! I won't say it again," Kareema yelled.

"Shawn, either shoot this bitch or give D-Ball the gun and let him do it." Jamal practically begged.

"You past that gun to his ass and I'll blow his fucking scalp off before he even reaches for it. Try me!"

"Shawn, listen to me…" Jamal said.

Shawn looked at Jamal and then looked at Kareema. He had a flash back from more than ten years ago when they were in a similar situation that resulted in Jamal getting shot. He didn't want that to happen again.

"I'ma count to three," Kareema warned. "One…"

"Shawn, shoot her! What the fuck are you waiting for? That's your fucking brother, nigga! Shoot that bitch!!" D-Ball yelled.

"Two!" Kareema yelled.

"Shawn! What the fuck!?" Maurice exclaimed as his heart raced. He looked from Jamal to Shawn.

"Shawn…" Jamal pleaded.

"Jamal!" Shawn yelled.

"Three!" Kareema screamed. Shawn pulled the trigger and a loud boom sounded off in the night.

Jamal and Kareema fell to the ground and the kick back from the gun made Shawn stagger back before falling to the ground as well.

"OH SHIT!!!" D-Ball and Maurice screamed.

Maurice turned his back and put his hands to his face. D-Ball was frozen, his heart in his throat. He breathed heavily afraid to move towards Jamal to see who was shot. Shawn trembled as he moved to his knees and crawled to his brother. He reached out a trembling hand and touched Jamal's ankle, shaking him.

"Jamal?" Shawn said in a shaky voice. Jamal didn't move so he shook him again. "Jamal?!" Shawn said louder as the tears began to come. Shawn was becoming frightened at the thought that he may have shot and killed his own brother.

D-Ball took a couple of nervous steps towards Jamal and Kareema to get a closer look. He closed his eyes and sighed deeply.

"Shawn…you didn't hit Jamal. You hit Kareema. Damn nigga, you got a muthafucking head shot off!" D-Ball yelled. He shook Jamal harder. Jamal blinked and opened his eyes a little. His body was sore from the two gunshot wounds he sustained. He looked at Shawn and managed to give him thumbs up. Shawn was visibly shaken. He put his head down and closed his eyes tightly as the tears came. He wasn't a trained killer, and he wasn't heartless enough to kill. But to save his brother, he did what he had to do. The roaring boom from the sound of the gunshot still echoed in his ears. He shook his head as he asked God to forgive him for taking a life but thanked God for giving him the strength to save his brother.

Maurice dialed 9-11. "Yeah, I need an ambulance at Darby Creek Trestle not too far from the Sharon Hill Trolley Line. We have three gunshot victims; one is a woman who is dead. Another is a man, I'm not too sure about his situation and we have an officer down… Yes, Detective Jamal Williams has been shot twice. We need help right away." Maurice disconnected the call and looked down at Shawn. He could tell that Shawn was shaken up over what happened. He put his hand on Shawn's shoulder and squeezed. It had been a hell of a couple of weeks for all of them. Unfortunately, Samir was still on the loose.

32

Jamal was rushed to a nearby hospital. Though Shawn felt horrible at the fact that he killed a woman, because he saved a cop, he was revered a hero. Once it was learned that he was Shawn Williams, basketball playing superstar of the Cimberio Varese Basketball team in Italy, every local newspaper and radio station wanted to interview him.

Though they weren't able to take Samir out, standing up to him repeatedly when he came after them showed him that they weren't afraid of him and Samir back off… at least for the time being. Samir was never one to back down from any one person and he was not about to have Jamal and his friends put ideas in other people's heads that he was slipping. Eventually he was going to have to send a message to let the streets know he was still a force to be reckoned with and not one to be trifled with.

Shawn sent for Chanda and his children to come from Italy back to Philly so they could spend Thanksgiving with their families. She was elated that Shawn didn't get hurt but knew she needed to be with him in Philly so she could help him cope with the fact that he shot and killed someone and to also see her best friend, Deisha.

It had been five days before Deisha opened her eyes for the first time after being shot. Most days, Maurice would be in her room after work and would hold her hand while he rested his head on the edge of her hospital bed. The day she finally woke up, she looked at him for a moment before gently stroking the back of his head with her free hand. The tube in her mouth had been removed a couple of days before.

Maurice looked up at her and smiled. "Hey, Beautiful," he said to her.

Deisha smiled back, unable to speak due to her mouth being so dry.

Maurice ran his fingers through her hair and kissed her softly on her lips. "I love you," he said to her.

Deisha mouthed, "I love you, too." Maurice kissed her hand and laid his head against it, closing his eyes and thanking God that Deisha survived.

It took a lot of courage for Manny to go to the spot where Kiree hid his money. Unfortunately, Kiree didn't leave behind any children and did not have a girlfriend at the time of his murder. The agreement that he and Manny had was if anything were to happen to either of them, all of their money would go to Keisha and Kamir. Kiree's stash was in the couch cushions in his living room. Instead of it being the typical stuffing inside, it was rubber bands of money. Manny had no idea that Kiree was putting that much money away. By the time he finished counting out the money, it was over 250 thousand dollars.

Manny and Kiree used to talk about starting their own mentoring program for the younger males; a Basketball league in the Spring and Summer and a Football league in the Fall and Winter. Knowing how much his mother loved to cook, he decided he would use the money Kiree stashed and fulfill all of their dreams. He opened a soul food restaurant in the East Falls section of Philadelphia along with an upscale lounge. He named the restaurant after his mother; Becky's Heart & Soul Delicatessen. The lounge was named after Manny and Kiree; K-E Sports Bar and Lounge, for Kiree and Emmanuel. Business boomed for both of his places of business and he officially retired from hustling.

D-Ball's plans to leave Philly were cancelled when Jamal offered him a deal that he couldn't refuse. He had D-Ball's record expunged as long as he agreed to join the police force. With his pull, he was able to help

D-Ball move up the ranks and become a detective in a very short time. Jamal never went back to Delaware. Instead, he stayed in Philly taking a permanent position that was offered to him after he was released from the hospital.

After returning to work, Keisha was talking with her co-worker Elizabeth who was sharing one of her many disappointing stories of a date that had went terribly wrong when she had a great idea. Since D-Ball was single and Elizabeth was single, she decided to set them up on a date with each other. She wasn't surprised that they hit it off with each other with their one date evolving into a steamy romance.

Though she refused to join a support group for rape victims, Keisha took time out to have private sessions with Deisha who helped her deal with the sexual assault and move on with her life. In return for the free sessions, Keisha shared her story with Deisha's teen patient, who had been molested by her stepfather, and convinced her to press charges so he could be put away for sexual abuse.

Samir was sitting in his office one evening after handling business with some of his associates. He was engrossed in a magazine that he was reading to waste time before heading out with a new female companion he was casually seeing when he happened to look up. A man stood in the door way of his office but Samir could not see his face fully due to how dimly lit his office was.

"Can I help you?" he asked, trying not to be annoyed. He was used to guys coming in looking for work, trying to wheel and deal, offering their services in exchange for his help.

"Long times no see, Samir," the unknown man said from the door.

"Do I know you?" Samir asked, now becoming annoyed.

"Yeah, you know me. You might not remember me. But you know me very well."

"Look, state your name and your business or get the fuck out of my office. I don't have time for kiddy games or riddles and shit," Samir said maliciously.

The unknown man stepped forward so Samir could see him fully. Samir looked at him for a long time with his mouth hanging open. The man smiled at Samir's reaction. "Do you remember me, now?" he asked with a look of malice on his face.

"What the..?" Samir started to say as his heart pounded in his chest. He couldn't believe his eyes. It was no way possible that this man could be standing in his doorway after all of this time. Normally, Samir did not fear anything or anyone. But laying eyes on this man struck fear in him all the way down to his core.

The unknown man pulled a gun and aimed it at Samir. "You don't know how fucking long I waited for this shit." Before Samir could say anything, the unknown man pulled the trigger three times quickly, shooting Samir twice in the chest and then a fatal shot to his head. He smiled down at his victim and left as quickly and quietly as he came.

Epilogue: The Unknown Man

Jamal couldn't believe his ears when he got the call at the police station telling him that Samir had been shot and killed. On the one hand, he felt sorrow and on the other hand he was elated that Samir had finally been taken out. He secretly wished he had been the one to do it. Jamal wondered who finally got the upper hand on Samir and caught him slipping. He tried to tell himself that it didn't matter but he still couldn't stop wondering. Since the murder happened out of his district, and because he was family, he couldn't sit in on the investigation. He called over to the area's precinct and asked one of the officers to give him any information that came in about Samir's murder. Being his cousin made it easy for him to make that request.

He was sitting at his desk looking over some files for a case that he and D-Ball were working on when an officer came over to him.

"Detective Williams?" the officer asked.

"Yes, that's me. What can I do for you?" Jamal asked as he looked up from his paper work.

"This just came in for you in regards to Samir Muhammad's murder. I was told to bring them to your attention."

Jamal took the closed manila envelope. "Do you know what this is?" he asked as he began opening it.

"Although there weren't any witnesses to Muhammad's murder, he did have security cameras around and they caught a man who was seen coming and leaving around the time of the murder. Hopefully that will give them some leads," the rookie officer explained.

"Okay," Jamal replied quietly as he took the images out of the envelope. "Thanks." The rookie cop left just as D-Ball was coming over to Jamal's desk. While in the office, Jamal called him Dante. D-Ball just didn't sound professional and Smith sounded too much like an insult. "Dante, what's good?" Jamal asked as he looked at the images that were given to him.

"We've got a homicide over on 29th and Dauphin. Looks like it stemmed from an earlier fight according to some of the witnesses," Dante said to him.

Jamal came across the next to the last picture and froze. He stared at the photo for a long time making sure his eyes weren't deceiving him. He thought he recognized the person in the photo. "That can't be..."

Jamal said quietly as he continued to stare at the individual.

"What can't be? What's up?" Dante asked when he noticed the perplexed look on Jamal's face. Jamal didn't hear him because he was too focused on the person in the photo. His heart raced and his palms began to sweat as he breathed deeply. "Jamal?" Dante called to him. "What's up with the picture?"

Jamal stared at it a little longer and then looked up at Dante. "I think I know who this is…" he said before looking at it again.

Dante came around to where Jamal was sitting and looked at the photo. He didn't recognize the person. "Okay, so who is it?"

Jamal looked at Dante and swallowed past a knot of fear in his throat. "My father…"

Ms. Keyona was bringing out a large green trash bag from her house to put onto the side walk. She didn't notice the man standing across the street watching her as he smoked a cigarette. He watched her for a long time, wanting so badly to go over to her and hug her, touch her hair, smell her skin, kiss her lips. But he knew that he couldn't. He took one last drag off of his cigarette and flicked it into the street before turning to walk away.

Ms. Keyona had a strange feeling that someone was watching her. She turned back around towards where the man was standing but didn't see anyone. She looked around and dismissed the feeling before opening her storm door. She noticed she had an envelope in her mailbox and took it out. She froze when she saw the handwriting, recognizing it from the many love letters that were exchanged between the two of them. Her hands shook as she read the brief note:

Keys, not a day has gone by that I didn't think of you or missed you, or thought of our sons. I can't explain things right now, but I will soon enough.

Forever and always, Dre.

"Oh my God…" Ms. Keyona mumbled as the tears fell from her eyes. She looked around frantically to see if she saw anyone nearby. She then looked at the envelope that the letter was in and was disappointed to see that there was no return address. She read the brief note again and again wondering how it could be possible. Andre was alive. But how…?

The End…?

A Thug's Redemption 3: The Wrath of Andre

Coming soon!

www.ingramcontent.com/pod-product-compliance
Lightning Source LLC
Chambersburg PA
CBHW060947120726
47910CB00002B/520